Well-chewed Homework!

I reached into my desk to pull out my math assignment. It looked like a lace doily! I stood up slowly, holding the tattered paper in front of me.

"Oh, dear," I heard Madame Pong whisper.

"For heaven's sakes, Rod," snapped Miss Maloney. "Where's your assignment?"

I swallowed hard, wishing I could lie.

"Rod?"

Glancing down at my desk, blushing, I mumbled, "Aliens ate my homework, Miss Maloney."

Books by Bruce Coville

Camp Haunted Hills Books:
How I Survived My Summer Vacation
Some of My Best Friends Are Monsters
The Dinosaur That Followed Me Home

Magic Shop Books:
The Monster's Ring
Jeremy Thatcher, Dragon Hatcher
Jennifer Murdley's Toad

My Teacher Books:
My Teacher Is an Alien
My Teacher Fried My Brains
My Teacher Glows in the Dark
My Teacher Flunked the Planet

Aliens Ate My Homework

Goblins in the Castle

Monster of the Year

Space Brat
Space Brat 2: Blork's Evil Twin

Available from MINSTREL Books

A MINSTREL PAPERBACK *ORIGINAL*

A Minstrel Book published by
POCKET BOOKS, a division of Simon & Schuster Inc.
1230 Avenue of the Americas, New York, NY 10020

ISBN: 0-671-88685-1

First Minstrel Books printing October 1993

10 9 8 7 6 5 4 3 2 1

Cover art by Stephen Peringer

Printed in the U.S.A.

ALIENS ATE MY HOMEWORK

BRUCE COVILLE

Interior illustrations by
Katherine Coville

PUBLISHED BY POCKET BOOKS

New York London Toronto Sydney Tokyo Singapore

For Mike,
With fond memories of summer nights
spent watching for aliens

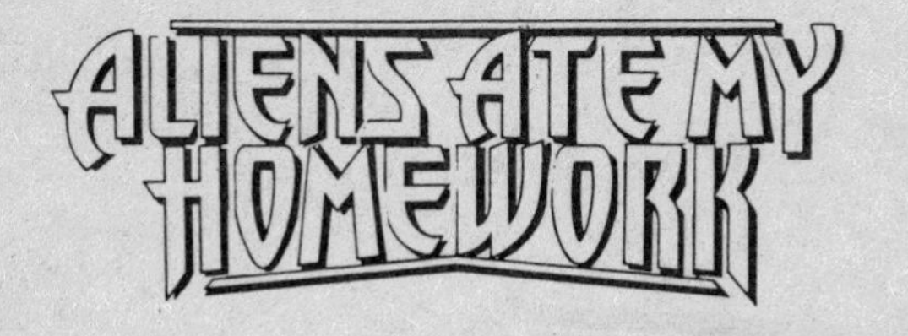
ALIENS ATE MY
HOMEWORK

CHAPTER 1

Billy Becker, Boy Beast

"WATCH OUT, PUDGE-BOY! HERE COMES NUMBER twenty-three!"

That was Billy Becker.

"Splat! Squish!"

That was Arnie Markle, providing sound effects for the final moments of the bug Billy was smushing against the back of my head.

"Mmmph grrgle!"

That was me, Rod Allbright, trying to say, "Let me go!"—which wasn't easy with Arnie sitting on my back and pressing my face into the grass.

Why was Billy Becker squashing a bug against the back of my head?

It was his hobby.

You know how it is: Some people collect stamps, or comic books, or beer bottle caps. Billy was collecting a list of how many kinds of bugs he could mash in my hair.

Why was Arnie helping him? Well, until Billy moved to town, Arnie had been our official class bully and kid most likely to spend time in prison. Then Billy got here, and within a month he had made it a point to beat up every boy in the sixth grade. What made this remarkable was that he was the smallest kid in the class—at least six inches shorter than most of us. My mother, who sort of drips sympathy, said she thought Billy was acting so tough to make up for his size.

Whatever the reason for Billy's bullying, most of the guys just stayed away from him after that first month. The only exception was Arnie, who was at least six inches *taller* than most of us and had been so awed by Billy's fighting skills that he became devoted to him. Now he was Billy's official hench-thug. This meant, among other things, that it was his job to hold me down while Billy smeared bugs in my hair.

"Okay, Arnie," said Billy, "you can let him up now."

I scrambled to my feet but didn't say anything; I had already learned what a mistake that could be. Arnie, unfortunately, was perfectly willing to talk. "I don't think that one should count," he said.

"Why not?" demanded Billy.

"It was a spider. Spiders aren't bugs."

Billy slapped his hand against his forehead. "How could I have been so stupid! I'm sorry, Pudge-Boy. Really. I'll tell you what. Just scratch that one off the list. And don't worry about it—I'll find something nice and juicy to replace it."

Snickering at their wit, Billy and Arnie wandered off.

My best friend, Mickey, helped me to my feet. Mickey had been the shortest kid in the sixth

grade until Billy showed up. He was still one of the nicest—which shows you what my mother's theory was worth. "I'm amazed," he said now.

"Why?" I asked as I dug for my comb. (I never used to carry a comb, but after Billy started his new hobby, I found it very useful for getting the bug guts out of my hair.)

Mickey shrugged. "That was the most intelligent thing Arnie's said all year."

You might wonder why I didn't just pound Billy's face in when he did these things—especially since he was so much smaller than me. The answer is simple: while Billy had already beaten up every boy—and half the girls—in the class, I, personally, had never managed to beat up anyone. The sad truth is, I'm not much good at anything physical. That's why the other kids call me Rod the Clod. (Except Billy, of course; he calls me Pudge-Boy, which I don't think is really fair, since the doctor says I only need to lose ten or fifteen pounds to be the right weight.)

The few times I lost my temper and actually struck back at Billy, he either put on his innocent face—which teachers and other adults seem to find totally angelic—or else he beat the daylights out of me.

I know I am not a good fighter. Even so, it is

very embarrassing to get beat up by someone a foot shorter than I am.

I was still trying to think of a way to get revenge on Billy when the afternoon bus dropped Mickey and me in front of our houses. We live about four miles out of town, and there are not a lot of other kids around, except for our stupid "siblings" (as our teacher, Miss Maloney, calls them). Mickey has one sibling and I have two. Mickey's is a little sister named Markie. She is pretty much a normal kid.

Mine are a matched set, three-year-old twins known as Little Thing One and Little Thing Two. They are not normal by any stretch of the imagination.

Their real names are Linda and Eric. They decided they wanted to be Little Thing One and Little Thing Two after I read *The Cat in the Hat* to them. (They had a fight about who got to be Thing One, but since Linda was born first, Eric was doomed to lose that battle. He loses a lot of fights that way.)

My mother is totally unamused by these names, but she can't do much about them because (a) they were the Things' idea, and (b) the Things are only three years old. (In case you don't happen to have any around, let me explain that three-year-olds are very good at insisting on this kind of thing.)

My dog, Bonehead, started barking as I came up the driveway.

"Hello, Rod, pick up your feet," said Mom as I stumbled over the doorstep. "I'm glad you're here. Mrs. Nesbitt needs help, and I don't want to take Eric and Linda over there if I don't have to."

"My name isn't Eric," said Eric without looking up from the blue finger paint he was smearing across a big piece of paper. "It's Little Thing Two. And I like Mrs. Nesbitt. She gives me cookies."

Mrs. Nesbitt is this old lady who goes to our church. Mom sort of watches out for her, which takes a lot of time.

Once I asked Mom why she did it. She just looked at me funny and said, "It needs to be done."

I wouldn't have cared all that much, except watching out for Mrs. Nesbitt didn't just mean extra work for Mom. (I mean, who do you think got stuck with Thing One and Thing Two while Mom was off playing Good Samaritan?)

"Can't you take them with you?" I asked. "I have to work on my volcano."

"The twins make Mrs. Nesbitt nervous."

"They make me nervous, too," I said. I started breathing fast and wheezing to prove it.

Mom gave me one of her looks. You know the kind I mean.

"All right," I muttered. "I'll do it."

Like I had a choice."

I decided to let the Things help me with the volcano—or at least, with making the papier-mâché I needed for the next step. The volcano was my project for the big end-of-the-year Science Fair, which was scheduled for that Friday. I had been working on it for over a week now, and it was going to be big time—a great-looking volcano that would really erupt when it was finished. I needed to add one more layer of papier-mâché before I could start painting it.

"Hey, kids!" I yelled as Mom headed out of the driveway. "Wanna make pooper mucky?"

("Pooper mucky" is what the Things called papier-mâché.)

"Yay for Roddie!" cried Little Thing One, who loved gooping around with the stuff.

Little Thing Two started to clap.

"Okay, you two get the tub. I'll meet you in my room."

It was one of those hot days that sometimes surprise you in early May, so I opened my windows and put on a pair of shorts. After spreading some papers on the floor to protect it from the goop we were about to make, I went to look at the volcano, which stood on a card table in the corner of the room. It was nearly two and a half feet high, built on a four-foot by four-foot square of plywood I had found in the basement. I was really proud of it.

The Things lugged in the tub we used for making papier-mâché, and we dumped in some torn-up paper left from the last time we had done this. Then I poured in water and paste, and we started squeezing it with our hands to get that nice oozy goop that is so much fun to work with. When it was pretty much ready, I went back to the volcano to see where I wanted to start working. Suddenly I heard a tearing sound. Before I could turn to see what had caused it, a dollop of papier-mâché smacked against the back of my bare leg.

"Wow!" cried Little Thing One.

"Holy macaroni!" cried Little Thing Two.

I spun around.

The first thing I saw was a big hole in the window screen.

The next thing I saw was globs of papier-mâché spattered all over the room, including a big splotch on Thing One's face.

The third thing I saw was a round spaceship

about a foot across that had landed in my vat of papier-mâché. I thought it must be a toy—until a blue glow began to crackle and sizzle around it. You could *smell* the electricity.

I revised my opinion. This thing was real!

The crackle continued. Just as I was wondering if the ship was going to explode, it started to grow.

Within seconds it was three feet long. I wondered if it was going to get so big it would blow our house to smithereens. But suddenly the crackling electric glow began to sputter. The ship shrank back to two feet, grew a bit, then shrank again. A moment later the crackling stopped.

The electric glow disappeared.

The spaceship held steady at about two feet.

Thing One and Thing Two had been edging closer to me while all this was going on. Now I had one of them clinging to each hand.

We waited, holding our breath.

Everything was silent.

We stepped forward, then stopped as a door opened in the side of the ship.

CHAPTER 2

Grakker

PART OF MY BRAIN WAS SCREAMING, "RUN, YOU fool! *Run!*"

Part of my brain was going, *This is the coolest thing that will ever happen to you in your entire life.*

My body, ignoring both parts of my brain, just shook.

A long ramp began to extend from the door of the ship. It stretched to the edge of the papier-mâché tub, then stopped.

A moment later a tiny green alien, two inches tall at the most, stepped onto the ramp. He had a body like Arnold Schwarzenegger and a face like a shaved gorilla. Little nubs, like baby horns, sprouted from his high forehead. His suit was brick red with gold trim at the neck and shoulders.

My first impulse was to pick him up. I think this was because he looked so much like the toys I had been playing with since I was the Things' age. Stepping forward, I reached out for him.

All right, all right—that was stupid. But I was feeling pretty addled at the moment. It didn't do anything to un-addle me when the alien pulled out a ray gun, pointed it at my head, and said, "One more move and I ventilate your skull."

Was this a sign that they hadn't come in peace? Or was it merely an indication of how stupid I had just been? It didn't matter. Raising my hands, I began to back away from the alien. After two steps I tripped and landed on my butt.

"Who are you?" I asked from my new position on the floor.

"My name is Grakker," said the little green guy. "I am the commander of this mission."

"What mission?"

"My crew and I are agents of the Galactic Patrol. We have been sent to this miserable, backward planet to capture a notorious criminal known and feared across the stars. Unfortunately"—and here he looked down at the vat of papier-mâché—"we seem to have encountered some difficulties. We will need your help. Therefore, I am making you a deputy."

"I beg your pardon?"

"Refused," said Grakker. "Provision 13.4.7.6 of the Galactic Legal Code gives me the right to deputize natives of underdeveloped planets in cases of emergency. If you resist, you may find yourself under arrest and heading for a trial on Alpha Centauri. Unless you want to spend the rest of your miserable little life pounding rocks on an asteroid, I would suggest you do as I say."

The guy was only two inches tall, but as long as he was holding that ray gun, he was as much of a bully as Billy Becker.

"I don't like him, Roddie," said Little Thing Two. "Make him go away."

"Silence, Larva!" snapped Grakker.

"Is he a Who?" asked Little Thing One. (I had read them *Horton Hears a Who* the night before.)

"Tell them to be silent!" ordered Grakker, pointing his ray gun in the general direction of right between my eyes.

"Can it, kids," I said softly. "I have to talk to the man."

"I want to play with him," said Little Thing One, stretching her pudgy, paste-covered hands toward Grakker.

"Back, Larva!" cried Grakker. He pulled the trigger on the ray gun. It made a tiny whining sound. A red light, no bigger around than one of those leads you use in an automatic pencil, hit the edge of the papier-mâché tub. After drilling a perfect, tiny hole right through the metal, it went on into the floor. It wasn't as easy to see, but I figured it was making a perfect tiny hole there, as well.

The hole really was tiny. But even a tiny hole that went all the way through your head could cause a lot of problems, like death.

"Linda, get back!" I snapped.

Thing One's lower lip began to tremble, and a big tear rolled down her cheek. "I want to play with him, Roddie," she whimpered, even as she backed up.

"Now see what you've done?" I said to Grakker.

Before he could answer, another alien came scuttling out of the ship. This one had yellow skin—at least, what I could see of it was yellow. Most of the new alien was covered by a sleeveless, high-collared robe that hung from its neck to its feet. The robe itself was blue, but I couldn't make out the exact shade because it kept shifting. Under the robe, which was open, was a long-sleeved tunic. The alien itself had a high bald head with big brow ridges (though not as big as Grakker's), a broad, flat nose, and huge pointed ears.

"Grakker, Grakker!" It sighed. "I knew you should have let me come out first. You're going to create a mess if you're not careful. At least let me change modules for you."

Something about the way this alien talked gave me my first hint that it was a female.

While Grakker muttered and grumbled, she reached a four-fingered hand up to the back of his head and pulled out something that would have been about the size of a very short pencil, if the aliens had been our size. After fumbling in her pocket for a moment, she produced another object about the same size and jammed it into the back of Grakker's skull.

Immediately he seemed to relax.

"Diplomatic module," said the second alien, looking at me and smiling. "Allow me to introduce myself—as I should have from the beginning." The last half of this sentence, spoken sharply, was directed more at Grakker than at me.

Grakker wrinkled his turned-up nose at her.

"My name is Madame Pong," said the second alien, turning back to me. "I am Diplomatic Officer for the good ship *Ferkel.*"

"I suppose you want me to take you to our leader?" I asked.

"Gracious, no!" she cried, her voice filled with horror. "We have no interest in establishing formal contact with your planet at this point."

"Why not?" I asked, wondering if I should be offended on behalf of all mankind.

"The time is not ripe," she said with a smile. "Now, while Grakker is correct that he can insist on your help, had it been I speaking, I would simply have requested it—as I will now. Would you help us, please?"

"What do you want me to do?"

"Simply remove our ship from this mess and take us someplace where we can enlarge it without destroying anything."

"How big is it going to get?" I asked nervously.

"Considerably bigger than this room," snapped Grakker, before Madame Pong could answer.

"Were you trying to enlarge it a minute ago?" I yelped, shuddering at the thought of what might have happened if they had succeeded.

Madame Pong's skin turned orange. "We were not aware that we had landed inside a dwelling. We are having some technical . . . problems." She glanced down at the papier-mâché. "My guess is that our sensing equipment has been clogged by this strange swamp."

"But you could have killed us!"

"We didn't," said Grakker, as if that made it all better.

"But you could have!"

"Will you take us outside, please?" asked Madame Pong, folding her hands in front of her and making a little bow. "Remember, we *do* need to enlarge the ship. It is in your best interest that we do so outdoors."

When she put it that way, I didn't have much choice.

"I'll have to bring the Things," I said.

Madame Pong looked puzzled, so I gestured to the twins.

"Perhaps my language program is defective," she said. "I did not think this culture referred to children as 'things.' "

"It's a long story. I'll tell you about it later, if you really want to know." I turned and headed for the door. "I'll be right back. I have to leave a note for my mother."

A beam of red light shot past my head and burned a tiny pit in the doorframe.

"Hey!" I cried, spinning around.

"I'm sorry, but you cannot leave this room unless I accompany you," said Grakker quietly.

I was surprised to hear him speak so politely—until I remembered the "diplomatic module" Madame Pong had jammed into the back of his head.

"Why not?"

"Security. For all I know, you're heading off to contact your government."

"They wouldn't listen."

"Nonetheless, I must accompany you."

I looked at Madame Pong. She nodded and said, "It is necessary."

"How do you want to do this?" I asked, remembering Grakker's reaction the last time I had reached for him.

"I'll ride on your shoulder."

Before I could ask if he wanted me to pick him up, he flew from the ramp of the ship to my shoulder.

"Rocket pack," he said when he saw the surprised look on my face. Settling to a sitting position on my shoulder, he pointed his ray gun at my head and added, "Don't try any funny stuff."

I nodded and headed for the kitchen. It took me a few minutes to find paper and pencil, but finally I left a note telling my mother I had taken the twins for a walk.

The delay made Grakker impatient, and he was muttering angrily as we started back toward my room. I thought maybe a little conversation would help calm him down, so I said, "Just how tall will you be when you get back to your normal size?"

"That is classified information," he replied fiercely.

I started to get mad. Then I thought, *If he wants to be that way, let him.* I shrugged, telling myself to ignore his rudeness.

Shouting with rage, Grakker scrambled up my collar. Grabbing the edge of my ear with one tiny hand, he poked his ray gun into my skin and shouted, "Freeze or fry, traitor!"

CHAPTER 3

Seldom Seen

I FROZE. I MEAN, WOULDN'T YOU?

"What is it?" I asked, trying to speak without moving my jaw. "What did I do?"

I sounded like a bad ventriloquist, but I didn't want to give Grakker any excuse to fire that ray gun.

"You tried to throw me to the ground," he said, sounding offended. "Fortunately, the trained reflexes of a Friskan fighter are more than a match for such an obvious move."

I started to ask what he meant, then realized my mistake. I suppose it should have been obvious: Never shrug while carrying a trigger-happy, paranoid alien on your shoulder.

Maybe they should add that to those survival rules your parents teach you when you're a little kid. ("Now, remember, Rod—don't eat soap, look both ways before you cross the street, and never annoy a temperamental alien.")

"Can I talk?" I asked in my bad ventriloquist voice.

"Softly."

"I wasn't trying to throw you off, I was shrugging. It's something we earthlings do."

"Do you expect me to believe that?"

"Why don't you ask Madame Pong?" I said. "Isn't she supposed to know that kind of thing?"

Grakker thought for a second, then said, "All right, we'll ask Madame Pong. But move slowly!"

"Look," I said as I walked *slowly* back to the room, "I'm not your enemy. I don't like the way you're treating me, but I'm not out to get you or anything."

"Just return to the room," said Grakker.

I hoped when we got back to the room, we wouldn't find the Things playing catch with the spaceship. If we did, I figured I could kiss my brain goodbye. Fortunately, Madame Pong had the situation well under control. The twins were sitting side by side, staring at her with fascination as she told them something I took to be a fairy tale from her planet. I expected Grakker to interrupt. To my surprise, he told me to be silent until she was done.

Before I could figure out what was actually happening in the story, Madame Pong said, "And *that* is how the snavel and the wonkus came to live happily ever after." Then she made one of her tiny bows.

The Things began to clap. "Tell it again," demanded Thing One.

"I'm sorry," said Madame Pong. "But, like the wonkus, I have work to do. Are you ready?" she asked, turning to Grakker and me.

I started to nod but thought better of it. "Yes," I said. (Did you know that if you have your lips apart, you can say "yes" without moving anything except your throat?)

We left through the back door. I had Madame Pong in my front pocket, the starship under my arm, and the Things and Bonehead bouncing along behind me. Grakker was still on my shoulder, pointing the ray gun at my head, despite the fact that I had assured him at least three times that I didn't have any intention of harming the ship.

"I am responsible for the safety of the *Ferkel*," he had replied each time. "Without meaning offense to you, I must do my job."

After the third time I had started to shrug but managed to stop myself.

* * *

Once we were outside, it took a few minutes to decide where to go. After all, when the ship expanded to full size, it was not going to be easy to hide. Fortunately, I had a lot of places to choose from. The land where my parents had built our house used to be part of Grampa's farm. The house sits on a hill that slopes down to a swamp. On the far side of the swamp lies a big field surrounded by woods. Grampa calls the field Seldom Seen. He gave it this name because the only way you can get to it is by going across the swamp—which you can only do on foot—or by making your way over a half mile of bumpy dirt road that cuts through a neighbor's automobile junkyard.

Seldom Seen is the only part of our land Grampa still uses; every spring he plants it with oats or corn. About the only people who ever go back there are my family, a few hired hands, and, in the fall, some hunters.

I love Seldom Seen and the woods that surround it. But I think the swamp is my favorite place because it's so odd, even spooky, with its murky pools and huge old willow trees.

To cross the swamp you start on this chunk of land that is usually dry—though it gets pretty squishy in the spring and the fall, sometimes actually ending up completely under water. Then you use this weird little bridge my father and some of his friends built, back when Dad was still around. The bridge is about six feet wide and twenty feet long; it has no side rails and is only about three feet above the water. Beneath it flows a stream, the only running water in the swamp. The bridge is a great place for lying on your belly and watching what swims underneath, which is mostly nothing, though sometimes in the spring there will be a big fish.

"A froggie!" cried Little Thing One as we started across the swamp. She loved frogs, and having spotted one, there was no way she was not going to chase it.

"Stop her, Bonehead," I cried, suddenly glad I had let him tag along. After all, I didn't dare chase Linda myself; any sudden movement might make Grakker trigger-happy. But if she got herself wet, I would be in big trouble with my mother.

Bonehead got her back into the group without much fuss.

"I like this," said Grakker as we stepped onto the bridge. "It looks like home."

"Do you come from a swamp planet?" I asked, thinking of some old movies I had seen.

"Do *you* come from a swamp planet?" he replied.

I started to ask what he meant, but then I figured it out on my own. A planet is a big place, and it's pretty silly to think it will be the same from one pole to another. That should have been obvious to me, since in this little walk we were going from lawn to swamp to field, and possibly to forest.

"I do not come from a swamp planet," said Grakker when I didn't answer. "But on my planet I used to live in a swamp." His voice was wistful, as if he was really missing his swamp. "It was a lovely place," he continued. "Boggy and smelly."

"How nice," I said.

"Don't get all soppy, Grakker," called Madame Pong from my pocket. "We have work to do."

I realized, to my surprise, that Grakker was sniffing.

"See any place big enough for the ship yet?" I asked, hauling Little Thing Two away from the edge of the bridge.

"Not yet," said Grakker. "Keep going."

"So how is it that you two speak my language?" I asked. "Did they give you a crash course before you left?" (I realized after I said it that under the circumstances "crash course" was a bad choice of words.)

"We have monitored your broadcast material for several decades now," said Madame Pong.

"That material is run through a computer, which analyzes your language. That analysis is used to prepare a language module, which we plug into a unit that has been surgically implanted in our brains. This module provides, within certain limitations, instant translations. If I take it out"—and here she reached up and pulled something from behind her ear—"grakkim spekk bribble eep eep!" she said, finishing the sentence with a couple of squeaks.

She replaced the module and said, "Simple, really."

"Elementary," I replied.

"I recognize that," said Madame Pong. "You're quoting Sherlock Holmes. I like Sherlock Holmes."

"How do you know about him?" I asked.

"I told you, we have been monitoring your broadcasts."

"So what do you think of what you've seen?" I asked, wondering if they had picked up things like "Gilligan's Island" and laxative commercials.

"You are a very troubled people," replied Madame Pong seriously. "We feel bad for you."

Before I could figure out what, if anything, to say to this, Grakker shouted (as loud as he could, considering that he was only two inches high), "There! That's the spot!"

We had left the swamp path and crossed the edge of Seldom Seen. Grampa had been plowing last week, so what we saw as we came out from between the scrub trees was eight acres of soft brown soil, surrounded on all sides by low-growing forest. Lots of room, no one to see—it was indeed perfect for the aliens' purpose.

"Walk on a bit," said Grakker. "We need to set the ship farther from the trees before we enlarge it."

"I wanna carry the spaceship, Roddie," said Thing Two.

"No, I wanna carry it!" whined Thing One, who clearly had not had a bit of interest in carrying it until just this moment.

"I have to carry it!" I said firmly before Grakker could jump into the battle. "And that's that."

"Strange species," said Grakker, "letting such undeveloped creatures walk around on their own."

"They're fun!" I said, defending the twins in spite of myself.

"Strange species," repeated Grakker. "Put the ship down here, please."

Following his directions, I placed the ship carefully on the ground. "Now what?" I whispered.

"Now we blow it up," said Grakker, causing

me to wonder if their language implants were as effective as they thought. "Move back."

I took the twins by the hands and walked back until Grakker said we were safe. After a moment a blue crackling light surrounded the ship.

"Wowie!" cried Eric as the ship began to grow. It doubled in size, then doubled again, until it was nearly ten feet across. Suddenly the crackling light began to fizz. We heard a series of loud bangs, like a string of firecrackers going off, followed by a whining sound as the ship shrank back to its two-foot size.

"Boogers!" said Grakker, which made me wonder again about his language module.

"Should we go over to it?" I asked nervously.

"Not yet," he said. "Let me talk to the people inside."

I was about to ask how he was going to do that when I realized he probably had some sort of radio equipment. I also wondered just how many aliens there were inside the ship. Two? A dozen? A hundred? This was starting to feel like a genuine invasion.

He pressed a button on his collar and began to mutter. After a while he stopped and bent his head as if listening. Mutter mutter, listen listen. Finally he pressed the button again, then turned to me and said, "We'll have to go back to your room. Something is wrong with the Enlarging Device, and we have to repair it. It looks as if we're going to be your guests for a while."

"What Grakker means," said Madame Pong, "is we would appreciate it if you would extend us your hospitality until we are able to repair our ship."

"What I mean," said Grakker, "is that he takes us back to the house and finds a safe place for us, or I arrest him for obstructing interplanetary justice."

CHAPTER

4

In Which I Become an Interstellar Criminal

MOM WAS BACK FROM TAKING CARE OF MRS. NESbitt, and she was not amused. Again. "Rod, you *know* I don't like you going off this close to suppertime," she said as I followed the twins and Bonehead through the door. "Where have you been?"

"We went back to Seldom Seen for a few minutes."

"With the aliens!" added Thing One happily.

Mom raised an eyebrow. "New game?"

"Sort of. The Things like it better than I do."

She smiled. "Well, I wish you hadn't gone out there right now. But I do appreciate your playing with them, Rod."

I felt pretty guilty, until I realized that even though I hadn't really been playing with the twins, if it hadn't been for me, the two of them might have tried playing with the *ship*—in which case Grakker might have melted them or something. So I had probably saved their lives.

"Where did you get that spaceship, anyway?" asked Mom, noticing what I was carrying.

Since I can't lie, it's not easy for me to answer a question like this. I thought fast. "I'm taking care of it for a friend," I said at last. Which was true, if I was willing to consider Grakker a friend!

"Well, be careful of it. You know I don't like you borrowing toys."

"I'll be *very* careful," I said sincerely.

Then, to my relief, she shanghaied the twins and marched them off to get ready for supper.

"I wanna play with the aliens!" wailed Eric as he disappeared into the bathroom.

I hightailed it for my own room. Once we were inside, Grakker and Madame Pong climbed out of my shirt pocket and used their rocket belts to fly down to my desk.

"Why is it so important to keep you a secret?" I asked.

"Your planet has not yet been approved for entry into the League of Worlds," said Madame

Pong, putting her hands together and making a little bow.

"Probably never will be," added Grakker.

Madame Pong reached behind Grakker and gave him a solid whack at the base of the skull. "Please forgive the captain," she said. "I fear that the diplomatic module I provided for him is not fully functional."

"But is what he said true? They *won't* let us into the League of Worlds?" I felt like I was being told about a club that I couldn't join.

"Let's just say that the matter is under discussion," said Madame Pong smoothly.

"As for us staying secret," added Grakker, "let me explain it this way. I am now giving you a direct order not to tell people about us. If you do not obey, you will be in violation of Galactic Ordinance 143.5.7.6. The penalties can be severe!"

"I'm just a kid! Why are you threatening me?"

"I'm not threatening," said Grakker. "I'm explaining. Madame Pong does not always understand the difference," he added as the diplomatic officer began to object.

Just then the phone rang.

"Rod!" called my mother after a second. "It's Mickey. He wants to talk to you."

I looked at Grakker. Would he let me answer

the phone, or was I being held prisoner in my own room?

"Better answer it," said Madame Pong, without giving Grakker a chance to forbid me.

I went out into the hall, which meant that I could talk without the aliens hearing me.

"Hey, Rod," said Mickey. "Is it okay if I come over?"

"It might be better if I came over to your place."

"How come?"

"This isn't a good time."

That was all Mickey needed to know. Sometimes it wasn't a good time at my house, sometimes it wasn't a good time at his house. He knew I'd fill him in later if I wanted to.

"I'll check with my mom," he said.

While Mickey was checking with his mom, I checked with mine.

"Not until after supper," she said, which was pretty much what I expected. I thought about checking with Grakker, too, but decided against it; I wasn't going to let him run my life any more than I had to. I would just lock the twins out of the room so they couldn't cause any trouble, and leave the aliens to fix their ship.

You might wonder why I was going over to Mickey's instead of staying to talk to the aliens.

The answer was simple. If I didn't tell someone about this, I thought I would explode.

Supper was Mom's famous tuna noodle casseroodle, which I actually like, strange as that might sound. Even so, I ate as quickly as I could without getting yelled at.

When I was done eating, I went to my room and locked it from the outside. (Mom had bought me a lock after the third time the twins had had "playtime" in my room while I was at school.)

I didn't tell the aliens where I was going.

As I went across the road to Mickey's house, I began to wonder if not telling the aliens was a mistake. But I knew that Grakker would simply have ordered me to stay home.

Mickey was waiting for me up in his room. I couldn't wait to get up there and tell him what had happened. But when I did, he didn't believe me!

I suppose that made sense. Who would? Besides, at the end of third grade we had started this game where we had a bunch of little alien friends. We used to sit outside at night and describe what they were doing in the sky above us. It was a lot of fun, but we had sort of stopped doing it in the last year. Now Mickey thought I was just trying to start a new version of it.

"I'm serious, Mick," I said, almost desperate. "I've got a tiny spaceship and at least two aliens in my room."

"Okay, then why don't you let me come over and see them?"

"I think they might kill me if I did."

I thought about that for a second after I said it. Would Grakker really kill me? Probably not. But I did think he was serious about taking me off to stand trial. I had a feeling he didn't believe in juvenile offender status.

Mickey started to laugh.

"Come on, Mickey. You know I never lie to you!"

"I know I never catch you," said Mickey, who loved to make up outrageous stories and see if he could get me to believe them. Once we were digging behind his house. We weren't digging for anything special, just digging, you know, to see how big a hole we could make. Anyway, we found this little blue bottle, and Mickey told me that it was magic and if I put water in it every day, eventually these famous people would come out of it.

This is probably the single stupidest thing I have ever believed, and I am not going to tell you how old I was when it happened because it is embarrassing. Let's just say that I was a lot younger than I am now, but also old enough that I should have known better. I think one reason I believed him was that since I can't lie, it is always hard for me to realize when someone else is lying to me.

"Look," I said, "I just became an interplanetary criminal by telling you this! I'm risking my life to let you in on this, and all you can do is make fun of me?"

By this time Mickey was laughing so hard he fell off his bed. "Stop it, Rod!" he gasped. "Please! I can't take any more."

You know how it is when people get laughing so hard that they can't stop? That's the way it was with Mickey. The more I tried to convince him that what I was saying was true, the more hilarious he thought it was. Finally his mother came up and sent me home because we were keeping his little sister awake.

It was dark outside, and a cold wind was blowing through the trees. It made me think of my father, because the last time I had seen him was on a night like this. I wondered where he was now.

When I got home, I had to go in and bop the Things good night. (They always want me to kiss them, which I do not want to do, so we have settled on a good-night bop, which I do softly with their teddy bears, Violet and Arnold.)

Next I kissed my mother good night. (I had tried to work out a bopping deal with her, but she still insists on a kiss.)

Finally I went to my room, where I figured I would have a long talk with the aliens. Now that I was used to the idea of what was going on, I was actually looking forward to this talk. I wanted to find out more about them, and where they came from.

That was before I walked through the door and discovered the disaster they had created. Then I wanted to kill them.

CHAPTER 5

Aliens Ate My Homework

"MY VOLCANO!" I CRIED IN DISMAY. "WHAT HAVE you done to my volcano?"

Actually, I didn't need to ask, I could see for myself. They had carved a huge pit in the front of it. I knew the aliens had done it, because Grakker was using his ray gun to slice out another chunk even as I watched.

There were five of them now: Grakker, Madame Pong, and three new ones, all of them on or near the volcano.

When the piece Grakker was working on came free, he passed it behind him to one of the new guys—a purple-brown creature who looked a little like a lizard in a blue cape. This guy dumped it into a big metal box that had a spout on one end. He was chanting nonsense syllables to himself as he worked.

Madame Pong stood above the pit, close to the top of the volcano, looking worried. Floating next to her was a potted plant that was slightly taller than she was. As near as I could tell, the plant was held up by little rockets mounted on the bottom of its pot. It had an enormous orange and yellow blossom—at least, enormous for a plant that was only a couple of inches tall. The blossom pointed slightly downward. A strange glow shone from behind the long petals.

The fifth alien stood at the control panel of another metal box. It had a body that was shaped something like a lemon. From the body came four legs, two arms, and a neck that was even longer than the arms. At the end of that long neck was a head that made me think of a turtle with bug-eyes. This alien was using one hand to punch buttons on the control panel; in the other hand it held a big chunk of my volcano. As I watched, it raised the chunk to its mouth and took a bite.

It was eating my science project!

"Stop!" I cried. "What do you think you're doing?"

"I have commandeered this structure for use

by the Galactic Patrol," said Grakker as he sliced off another chunk of volcano. "We require some convertible mass for energy purposes, and this material was the most suitable we could find. The molecular structure seems already to have been reduced to a simple level, which saves us a great deal of trouble."

"Besides," added the bug-eyed turtle, taking another bite, "the taste is most excellent. And it has much to nourish a warrior."

"I don't care if it's vitamin-enriched! That's my science project. I have to take it to school in two days!"

Grakker narrowed his eyes. "Are you claiming your project is more important than interplanetary justice?" he asked.

The lizard guy, the one who had been chanting, put his hand on Grakker's arm. "Careful, my captain," he whispered.

Grakker shook his hand away. "Are you saying this project is more important than the capture of a deadly criminal?"

At the moment I felt exactly that way. However, I knew that "Yes!" was not the answer Grakker had in mind.

"But my volcano . . ." I stammered.

"Rod, there are bigger things at stake here than your homework," said Madame Pong softly.

"Right now I would be happier if *we* were bigger," said the plant.

I blinked. "Did that thing just talk?"

"No, it was the wind rustling through my leaves."

"How do you do that?" I cried. "You don't even have a mouth!"

I immediately wondered if that was true. Who knew what might be hidden by those petals?

"Of course I don't have a mouth," said the plant.

"Then how do you talk?"

"Pod burps."

"I beg your pardon?"

Uncurling one of its dozens of tendrils, the plant pulled aside a leaf. With another tendril it pointed to a dark green pod hanging from one of its internal stems. "I suck air into the pod, then use it to burp out sound."

"Consider that a loose translation," added Madame Pong, a furrow wrinkling her high yellow brow. "*Burp* is probably not the most precise word. However, your language has no closer analog for the process."

"But it's a plant!" I said, none too intelligently.

"And you're meat," replied the plant. "Amazing that you can think at all, isn't it?" It paused, then waved several tendrils and added, "Or can you?"

Great. This alien plant not only talks, it's a wise guy!

"Where have you been, anyway?" asked Grakker. "I don't recall giving you permission to leave the area."

I had about had it. "You're not my boss!" I snapped.

"I am for the time being," said Grakker.

Suddenly he narrowed his eyes, which meant that they nearly disappeared under that great beetling brow of his. Turning his ray gun from the volcano toward me, he said, "You didn't tell anyone about us, did you?"

I've heard that things which happen early in your life can have a deep effect on you. I suppose that's why I can't lie.

It happened when I was about three, which was back when my dad still lived with us. Mom had made some of her special chocolate cookies. I loved these cookies. Well, actually, I never met a cookie I didn't like, which is one reason I am pudgier than I would like to be. But these were Mom's specialty, and I loved them—despite the fact that they were kind of dry and could suck the moisture out of your mouth quicker than a sponge.

Anyway, I had asked if I could have one, and Mom had said no. I had decided I wanted one anyway (remember, I was only three years old), so I snuck into the kitchen, took a chair from the table, and used it to climb onto the counter. Then I crawled over to the cookie jar, opened the top, and took out one of the chocolate treasures I had been longing for.

Suddenly I heard my mother coming!

I started to crawl back along the counter. Not fast enough . . . she was going to enter the kitchen before I could get away. I would be caught, chocolate-handed, so to speak.

I did the only thing I could think of to get rid of the evidence.

I crammed the entire cookie into my mouth.

When my mother walked into the kitchen she found me crawling along the counter, eyes wide, cheeks bulging.

It didn't take a Sherlock Holmes to see what I had been doing.

"Rod," she asked softly, "do you have a cookie in your mouth?"

Do you know what I did?

I denied it! Right in front of her, with my mouth full of cookie, I said, "No!"

At least, I tried to. But remember, these cookies were real saliva suckers. My mouth was drier than a three-day-old peanut butter sandwich. When I tried to say, "No, I don't have a cookie in my mouth," what came out was a spray of chocolate crumbs and the words, *"Mmmph, nngo hmmmana keee mimou!"*

Under the circumstances, it was unlikely that Mom was going to believe me.

I was made to stand in a chair facing the wall for half an hour. Mom stressed that the reason she was punishing me was not so much that I had taken the cookie, but that I had lied to her.

That was the last time I ever lied.

As I said, things that happen to you early on tend to have a deep effect.

It wasn't just that I didn't want to lie, or that I thought it was wrong. I just plain couldn't do it. If someone looked at me and asked me a direct question, they got the truth.

However, most people asking me questions I did not want to answer were not also pointing ray guns at my head. The situation at the moment was something different than I had ever faced before.

"Well," growled Grakker, "did you tell anyone about us?"

I swallowed, hard. My mouth was as dry as cotton.

I could almost taste that old chocolate cookie.

"Yes," I said unhappily, "I told someone."

"Grakker!" cried Madame Pong. "Don't!"

She was too late. He raised his ray gun, pointed it at me, and fired.

CHAPTER 6

Aliens in My Backpack

IF GRAKKER HAD SWEPT THE RAY FROM SIDE TO SIDE, I think I would have been dead. But he held the gun steady, which meant the beam hit me in only one place: my right ear.

"Ouch!" I cried, slapping my hand to the side of my head. "That hurt!"

Which shows, I suppose, how quickly people can shift mind-sets. Two seconds earlier I had been expecting to die; now I was complaining because my ear hurt.

"Consider it a warning," snapped Grakker. "And try not to make me hurt you any more than I already have. It is hard to say how much damage you have caused with your flapping foodsucker. If our quarry escapes, I may take you back to stand trial in his place."

Ignoring the tiny tyrant, I went to check my wound in the mirror that hangs over my dresser. I stared at my reflection for a moment, then blinked in dismay. Grakker had burned a tiny, bloodless hole straight through the lobe!

"You pierced my ear! Mom is going to kill me for this!"

"Thank her for saving me the trouble."

"What am I going to tell her?" I moaned.

"You could try the truth," said Grakker, turning his ray gun back to my volcano. "But I wouldn't suggest it, unless you want to see what happens when you really break the rules."

I groaned and turned back to the mirror.

"Rod," said Madame Pong gently, "I'm wondering if you can tell us anything about BKR."

(She pronounced it "Bee Kay Are," but later they told me that BKR was the most accurate way to write it.)

"Never heard of it," I said.

"It's not an it, it's a him," said the long-necked alien.

"Well, then, I never heard of *him*. Who is he?"

"The vicious bud-plucker we've been sent here to capture," said the plant.

"Actually, I think he's going by another name here," said Madame Pong. "Wait a moment while I check my notes."

I expected her to fumble in her robe for a notepad or something. Instead, she pulled a wire from the metal band that circled her wrist. With one end of the wire still connected to her wrist, she stuck the other end into her ear.

She closed her eyes for a moment, then nodded.

"Yes," she said. "According to our spywork, BKR is hiding here under the name of Becker."

"Becker?" I cried. "Billy Becker's father is an *alien?*"

This was too good to be true, though it certainly explained a lot of things.

"How long has he been here?" I asked, wondering if Billy was half-alien himself, or if he had been adopted, or what.

Her eyes still closed, Madame Pong wrinkled her brow.

"Twelve of your years," she said.

"Twelve years?" I yelped. "What took you so long to get here?"

"Don't ask," growled Grakker. He sliced another chunk off my volcano and passed it to the alien operating the energy conversion machine.

"I take it you know this person?" asked the plant. After floating down the volcano to the level of the table, then across to the edge, it raised its blossom to point up at me. But it had folded its petals to cover the glowing center, so I still couldn't see what was inside.

"I know his kid. At least, I guess it's his kid. Do you think he really had a kid here, or did he just adopt him?"

"Hard to say," murmured Madame Pong, pulling the wire from her ear. "He is a wily opponent, and there is no telling what he might do. However, the child may be a good place to begin our investigation—especially while we are consigned to this miniature status. What do you think, Grakker?"

Grakker looked up at me and said, "Madame Pong and I will be going to school with you tomorrow. You will be responsible for our safety. If anything happens to us, you will be held personally accountable by the Galactic Patrol and will probably have to stand trial. The GP does not take loss of its agents lightly."

"Thanks," I said. "I'm sure I'll sleep better tonight knowing that."

The lizard-faced alien snorted, and Grakker frowned at him.

Ignoring Grakker, the long-nosed guy said, "I am Snout—at least, that is your language's version of my nickname. It has to do, as you can see, with my face. My real name is Flinge Iblik. I am the ship's Mental Officer."

"Is that like being the ship psychologist?" I asked.

"Don't answer!" snapped Grakker. "It's classified information."

Flinge Iblik—Snout—rolled his eyes. But he smiled, too, as if he was used to this kind of thing from Grakker and didn't take it too seriously.

Before he could say anything else, the four-legged alien waved his hand at me and said, "Greetings upon you, Earthchild. I am Tar Gibbons."

"Pleased to meet you," I said. "Should I call you Tar?"

"*Tar* is not a name," said Madame Pong. "It's an honorific—like Mister, or Doctor, or Professor."

"What does it mean?" I asked.

Tar Gibbons waved a hand. "Your language has no exact equivalent. In rough translation, it would be something like, 'Wise and beloved warrior who can kill me with his little finger if he should so desire.' "

"I see," I said nervously.

"And I am Phillogenous esk Piemondum," burped the plant. "But you can call me Phil."

I had a feeling the three new aliens would have been glad to take a break and have a little chat with me, but Grakker wasn't about to let that happen. "Back to work," he said. "We've got a lot to do here."

"I'm sorry, Rod," said Madame Pong. "Perhaps we can talk tomorrow."

I was too wound up—and too worried—to go to sleep. My head was spinning with questions. What if Billy Becker's father found out we were on to him? Would he come after me? Even more frightening, would he come after my family?

When she saw me tossing and turning, Madame Pong flew over to my bedside and began to sing to me.

Within moments I was sound asleep.

The twins proved very useful the next morning. Between the oatmeal war and Little Thing One flushing Little Thing Two's fluffy bunny down the toilet, my mother was so distracted that I was able to keep her from noticing my newly pierced ear. I didn't think I could keep it hidden forever, but for now I figured I had enough to deal with.

When I went back to my room after breakfast, Madame Pong handed me a small gold stud. "Put this in your ear," she said.

"Where did you get it?" I asked in astonishment, wondering if they had been out robbing jewelry stores while I slept.

"We made it."

"Out of some of this white stuff," added Phil, waving a tendril at my volcano.

"This doesn't look like papier-mâché," I said, looking at the stud.

"It's not," said Madame Pong. "We converted the basic matter into new elements. This is a transmitter."

"A transmitter?"

"Yes. Put it through the hole in your ear, and we'll be able to talk to you while we're in your backpack."

"Do you mind if I wait till we get outside?" I asked. "I don't want Mom to see it."

"Delaying the moment of truth is like holding back birth," said Snout, tweaking the end of his nose so that it wobbled up and down.

"I can live with that," I said.

Grakker had decided to bring Snout along, so I left for school with three aliens in my backpack. Tar Gibbons and Phil were going to try to fix the ship while we were gone.

"Hi, Rod," said Mickey when I met him at the bus stop. Then his eyes went wide. "Oh, wow! When did you get your ear pierced? I can't believe your mother let you do it."

"She didn't," I said.

"You're kidding! I can't believe you did it without telling her!"

"Neither can I," I replied with perfect honesty.

We had to wait outside the school doors until the official opening time. I always hated that because it was one of the times Billy Becker was most apt to pick on me. On the other hand, since the aliens wanted me to get them a close-up look at the little bully, this might be a good time for it.

I looked around. Billy was nowhere in sight.

I decided to check on the aliens. Opening my backpack, I peeked inside. The three of them were a little disheveled, but other than that they looked fine. Bending my head over the backpack, as if I was searching for something, I whispered, "How are you doing?"

Before they could answer, I felt a smack at the back of my head. "Official replacement for number twenty-three!" called Billy Becker gleefully.

Without thinking, I straightened up. Big mistake. Billy's pal Arnie was standing right there, too. Looking past me, he spotted the aliens.

"Hey, what's this?" he cried.

Before I could stop him, he plunged his hand into my backpack and pulled out Grakker.

CHAPTER 7

Action Figures

I HELD MY BREATH, WONDERING IF ARNIE WOULD squeeze Grakker until he popped—or if maybe Grakker would zap Arnie.

To my astonishment, *nothing* happened right away. When Arnie lifted the little alien to examine him, Grakker held so still he might as well have been made of plastic—which, as it turns out, was exactly what Arnie took to be the case.

"This little guy is pretty cool," he said admiringly. "Where'd you get him, Allbright?"

Can't lie. Didn't buy him. What to say?

I thought fast and told the basic truth: "I found him."

"Huh. I thought so. I lost one just like this yesterday."

And with that, Arnie stuffed Grakker into his jacket pocket!

"Hey!" I cried. "Give him back! He's mine!" (Okay, that last sentence wasn't strictly true; Grakker wasn't exactly *mine.* But you know what I meant.)

"You said you found him," said Arnie. "I'm telling you I lost him. Wanna make something of it?"

Before I could answer him, Madame Pong's voice sounded in my ear. "Rod, what's going on?"

"Later!" I snapped.

"Later?" sneered Arnie. "How about right now?"

"I wasn't talking to you," I said.

"Oh? Who were you talking to?"

What was I supposed to tell him? That I was talking to an alien? Stuck for an answer, I stood there like some kind of idiot.

"What a dweeb!" said Arnie. "Come on, Billy. Let's go."

The two creeps sauntered off. I considered chasing them and trying to get Grakker back. But the truth was, if I pushed things, Arnie was likely to end up with not only Grakker in his pocket, but Madame Pong and Snout as well. I decided it was better to retreat before things got worse.

Besides, I had a feeling that Grakker could take

care of himself. *I only wish I could say the same for me,* I thought as I dug my comb out of my pocket and started cleaning the remains of poor number twenty-three out of my hair.

"Are *those* the aliens you were telling me about last night?" asked Mickey after Arnie and Billy were out of earshot.

For a moment I thought he finally understood the truth. Then he asked where I had gotten them and how much they cost.

I sighed. "I found them," I repeated. "I don't think you can get them around here."

"Come on, Rod. I want some, too. They're the coolest action figures I've seen in a long time."

"I'm serious. No place around here sells them."

"Well, let me look at the others," he said, reaching toward my backpack.

"No!"

"All right, all right," he said, throwing up his hands. "Boy, are you touchy today."

Madame Pong's voice sounded in my ear again. "Tell him you're afraid that you'll lose the rest of us if you take us out of the pack."

Good idea!

"I'm not touchy," I said. "I'm just afraid Arnie and Billy might come back and steal the others if I take them out now."

Mickey sighed. But he knew what I said was true, so he backed off.

When school started I took Madame Pong and Snout out of my backpack and slipped them in my desk. Then I bent down and stared into the desk, pretending I was looking for something. This did not look suspicious, because I am always looking for something in my desk, which is usually pretty messy.

Between the books, crayons, toys, and crumpled papers, the poor aliens didn't have much room. The most embarrassing thing was the half-eaten sandwich that had gone moldy.

"If I had known you were coming, I would have cleaned house," I whispered, pulling out the sandwich so I could throw it away.

"Better to live as if company is always on the way," said Snout, bowing his head and nodding.

"You'd get along fine with my mother," I replied. Putting my hand into the side of the desk, as if I were digging for something, I moved my face even closer to the aliens and hissed, "What are we going to *do*?"

"I do not know," replied Madame Pong. She looked very worried. "This development endangers the mission. However, Grakker is very good at taking care of himself. Perhaps he will escape on his own. My greatest fear is that he will do something drastic. . . ."

Her voice trailed off. I put my finger to my earlobe. Grakker had pierced my ear just for *saying* too much. What would he do to Arnie if he got really desperate? Much as I disliked the kid, I didn't want him to end up dead.

On the other hand, Grakker was only two inches tall—and in the clutches of a kid who was *not* known for being careful with toys. Annoying as the little alien could be, I didn't want him to end up dead, either.

Before I could decide who was in more danger, Arnie or Grakker, I was interrupted by a hand on my shoulder. "Are you ready to stop playing and join us, Rod?" asked Miss Maloney.

"Sorry," I said, scrambling into my seat. Well, I tried to scramble into my seat. I missed by a couple of inches, slid to the floor, and had to try again. The rest of the class laughed. I would have blushed, but I was used to it by now. They don't call me "Rod the Clod" for nothing.

The morning passed slowly. I was so worried about Grakker I wasn't able to concentrate on what Miss Maloney was saying—which let me make a fool of myself at least twice that I can remember. By lunchtime I was really nervous. Would Arnie take Grakker to lunch with him? Would he do something dangerous or stupid? (His two specialties.) What would Grakker do to *me* if he got out of this?

As it turned out, Arnie's interest in Grakker was less in *having* him than in taking him away from me. So he didn't bother to bring him to lunch.

By the time we got back from the cafeteria, the little alien was no longer in Arnie's desk—he was back in mine.

When Arnie realized that his new "action figure" was missing, he looked at me suspiciously. But as I had been right in his sight all through lunch, it was clear I couldn't possibly have taken the alien out of his desk. And he couldn't complain to Miss Maloney, since ownership of the "toy" was not a matter he would particularly want to bring up.

Even though he couldn't figure out any way that I could have taken Grakker from his desk, I was sure Arnie would still assume it was my fault. I was equally sure I was going to pay for it at recess.

In that much I was right.

Recess didn't start out too badly. Madame Pong and Grakker wanted to stay in the room to investigate things while the class was outside. Grakker ordered Snout to come with me, to observe the playground action.

When no one was looking, I tucked the little guy in my front pocket, and he made amusing comments to me while Mickey and I sat on the monkey bars. Finally he made me laugh out loud while Mickey was telling me about getting in trouble with his father that morning.

"Well, I'm glad *you* think it's funny," he said, jumping down from the bars and walking away.

"Mickey, wait!" I yelled. "I didn't mean it!"

But he ran off to play with some other kids.

"I most humbly apologize," said Snout. "I did

not want to cause trouble between you and your friend."

"Don't worry," I said. "He gets sensitive sometimes. It won't last."

I was the one who should have been worrying. I got off the monkey bars and started to wander toward the building. As I walked, Snout started to tell me a little about his planet. I got so interested in what he was saying I didn't look where I was going. Major error. Next thing I knew Arnie and Billy had me cornered against a blank wall near the kindergarten rooms.

While it would normally have been Billy who took the role of torturer, today Arnie had a personal grievance against me. So it was Billy who kept an eye out for the teacher while Arnie pushed me against the wall and said, "Give it back, Allbright."

"Give what back?" I asked, trying to sound innocent.

"You know. That little monster guy. You took it out of my desk. I want it back."

"I didn't take anything out of your desk, Arnie. Honest."

Arnie looked at me funny. Even though he liked to beat me up, he knew I didn't ever lie.

"What are you trying to pull, Allbright?"

"Nothing! I'm just trying to get through the day without getting my face pounded in."

More truth.

"Well, better luck tomorrow," said Arnie, drawing back his fist.

I saw the punch heading straight for my face.

I was sure I was dead—or at least severely wounded.

Then time went all funny.

CHAPTER 8

Temporal Disruption

ARNIE'S FIST WAS HEADING STRAIGHT FOR MY NOSE. I could see it coming, inch by inch by inch, as if it were moving in slow motion. I was so boggled by what was happening I almost didn't realize that this was my chance to get out of the way.

Finally I ducked.

Arnie's fist shot past my shoulder and smashed into the wall. "Ow!" he screamed. "What'd you do that for, Allbright?"

Like it was my duty to stand there and let him cream me.

I got ready to run, figuring he was really going to get me now. Instead he started crying. That was when I noticed the blood streaming down his knuckles. Cradling his injured hand, he ran off toward Miss Maloney.

Billy Becker stared at me in astonishment. "How did you duck so fast?" he demanded.

"Look at all the practice I've had," I replied, wondering if he was going to beat me up on Arnie's behalf. But he just squinted at me for a minute, then turned and walked away.

Once Billy was gone I sat down against the wall. "What happened?" I whispered to Snout. "What did you do?"

"I am not the master of mental arts for nothing," he replied smugly. "That was an example of temporal disruption, one of my specialties."

"What does that mean?"

"I put you into a different time frame. In other words, I set things up so that time went more slowly for you than it did for your attacker. That gave you time to duck. It takes a great deal of energy, and I can't manage it for long. But it seemed a reasonable thing to do under the circumstances."

"I'm glad you're on my side."

"Don't be too glad," he replied. "Being on our side means that BKR is on the other side. He is a fierce enemy—and you seem to have enemies enough as it is." He paused, then added, "Perhaps we can help you with that while we're here."

And that is just what he did for the rest of the day. For example, as we were heading in from the playground, I got a message through the transmitter in my ear: "Enemy approaching from behind. Duck left."

As I stepped aside, Billy Becker went stumbling past with the next bug he had been planning to add to his collection. He looked so astonished and frustrated that I almost felt sorry for him. As I thought about it, I did kind of feel bad. After all, I knew something that he didn't. At least, I assumed he didn't know his father was an alien. *Or did he?* Was that why he acted so weird all the time? Whether he knew or not, he was still in for an awful surprise if Grakker and company were successful. If they had their way, his father would be headed for the interplanetary hoosegow.

Of course, it was possible that Billy and his mother would just stay here, and Billy would be worse than ever.

Now that was a revolting idea!

After recess we had math. Miss Maloney was starting a unit on dividing fractions, and it made almost no sense to me, until Madame Pong started sending me explanations through my transmitter. This wasn't so bad!

A couple of times I did have a problem understanding her because of some background noise. At first, I thought it was static. I finally realized what the noise had actually been when it came time to hand in my homework.

It was the sound of someone chewing!

What made me realize this was the fact that when I reached into my desk to pull out my math assignment, it looked like a lace doily. I stood up slowly, holding the tattered paper in front of me.

"Oh, dear," I heard Madame Pong whisper.

"For heaven's sakes, Rod," snapped Miss Maloney. "Where's your assignment?"

I swallowed hard, wishing I could lie.

"Rod?"

Glancing down at my desk, blushing, I mumbled, "Aliens ate my homework, Miss Maloney."

I wish I could get a laugh like that when I tell a joke! My cheeks burning with embarrassment, I slumped in my chair.

Grakker, of course, was furious. "Saying that we ate your homework was in direct contravention of my orders," he raged that afternoon, when we were back in my house.

"It was brilliant," said Madame Pong serenely.

Grakker turned to her in astonishment. "What do you mean?"

"What Snout did on the playground was likely to generate some suspicion. Rod's answer to his teacher sounded so absurd that it has distracted people from what is really happening. You might make a good diplomat, Rod," she added, turning to me. "The creative use of truth is one of the most important of our skills. Besides," she continued, turning back to Grakker, "if *you* had been able to control your appetite, the whole incident might have been avoided."

I had been wondering which one of them had actually eaten my math!

Grakker growled, but I could tell that Madame Pong had scored a heavy point.

The whole mess got put aside when Phil floated out of the *Ferkel* and said, "I think we've got it fixed. Let's go try her out."

The plan was that the aliens would fly back to Seldom Seen, enlarge the ship, and get on with their work.

I knelt in front of my desk. "I'm sorry about this afternoon," I said. "And I really did appreciate the help that you guys gave me dealing with Billy and Arnie."

"It was our duty," said Grakker gruffly. "After all, you are a deputy of the Galactic Patrol."

"It was our *pleasure,*" said Madame Pong firmly.

For some reason it felt better to think that they

had helped me because they liked me, rather than just because they *had* to.

"If all goes well, we will not see you again," said Grakker, his voice still stiff and formal. "Assuming that to be the case, let me thank you on behalf of the galaxy for the assistance you have rendered to date."

He stood for a moment, his big jaw grinding. Finally Madame Pong nudged him with her elbow.

With a sigh, he stretched out his hand and said, "Please accept this small token of our gratitude." On his palm rested a circle of some material about the color of my flesh.

"What is it?" I asked.

"A patch for the hole in your ear," said Madame Pong with a smile. "Here, let me put it on for you."

Taking the circle from Grakker's hand, she floated to my shoulder. Taking out the gold stud, she applied the patch to my ear. "There," she said, sounding satisfied. "Go look."

Madame Pong still on my shoulder, I went to my mirror. I stared at my ear in astonishment. You couldn't tell that anything had happened to it!

"Thanks!" I said, happily.

"It was the least we could do," said Madame Pong.

She flew back to join the others.

Grakker gave me a salute. I saluted back, feeling kind of funny about having the little guys leave. They had only been here for a day, and certainly they had been more trouble than anything else. Yet in a strange way it had been fun having them around. I had certainly liked having Snout foil Billy's bug-squashing attempt during recess.

Madame Pong made a bow to me. I bowed back.

The five of them climbed into the *Ferkel.*

"Wait until I open the window!" I cried.

Grakker's voice came through a speaker. "Hold flight until exit prepared," he said.

I opened the window. The ship shot past me. I watched it disappear among the trees of the swamp.

Then I lay down on my bed and stared at the ceiling.

I guess that old line about the best laid plans of mice and men applies to aliens too, because about fifteen minutes later the *Ferkel* flew back through my window. (It was a good thing I hadn't bothered to close it!)

The *Ferkel* landed on my desk. After a moment the ramp extended and Grakker stepped out. He was not a happy alien.

"What happened?" I asked.

"Nothing," he said tensely.

"Sorry, boss," said Phil, floating down the ramp after Grakker. He was waving his leaves and vines wildly about, as if trying to explain something. "I told you it might not work." Turning to me, the plant added, "We're missing a vital part. In your language it would be called—" he paused, and waved his leaves, as if thinking.

"I think the technical word is *doohickey,*" said Tar Gibbons. "Either that or *thingummy.* It's also known as the Focus/Diffusion Gizmo because it either focuses or diffuses the enlarging ray, depending on the size of the ship. Usually we just call it the F/D Gizmo."

"Right," said Phil. "The F/D Gizmo. Anyway, Tar Gibbons and I tried to create a replacement, but we didn't get it right. No surprise; these things are tricky. But Meathead here thinks it's an interplanetary crime."

I was astonished to hear Phil talk that way. Well, it was no surprise that he called Grakker a meathead; we were all meatheads from a plant's point of view. But I figured he would be required to show a little more respect for his commanding officer.

Madame Pong was next down the ramp. "I'm sorry, Rod," she said, bowing again. "It looks as if we'll have to ask your hospitality for another night."

I smiled. To my surprise, I was actually glad to have them back.

That night I worked on repairing the hole the aliens had made in my volcano while the aliens themselves worked on their ship. They told me stories while they worked. It was kind of cozy; reminded me of what it used to be like when my dad still lived with us.

Actually, I guess I started it when I asked Madame Pong a question about what she did. She responded by telling me this long story about growing up on her planet and having to harvest trailing wortmungle in order to earn money to go to school so that she could become a diplomat.

That got the rest of them reminiscing about their childhoods. It was funny the things they had in common, and the things that were different. For example, nearly all of them had had problems with their brothers and/or sisters.

"Family problems are universal," said Phil,

waving a leaf. "Take me. My brother was a real nut. And my sisters—what a bunch of fruits!"

Before I could figure out if he was joking, Tar Gibbons said, "I have no problems with brothers or sisters because I have none."

"Did you like being an only child?" I asked.

"Oh, I wasn't an only child. I had several siblings. Just no brothers or sisters."

"Wait a minute. Siblings are people who have the same parents as you do. So you had to have brothers or sisters."

"Brothers are male, correct?"

I nodded.

"And sisters are female?"

When I nodded again, Tar Gibbons spread his arms, leaned that long neck forward, blinked at me, and said, *"Then I don't have any."*

"Well, that just doesn't make sense!" I was starting to get a little angry because I thought he was teasing me.

"Why not?"

"They have to be one or the other!"

"Oh, don't be silly. I am neither male nor female. I'm a farfel."

"Is that more like a boy or more like a girl?"

"Actually, it's more like a pippik than anything."

I turned to Madame Pong, but she just spread

her hands. "I don't think you want to get into a discussion of biology as it is practiced on Tar Gibbons's planet."

"Okay," I said. "Just tell me what pronoun to use when I'm talking about him. Her. Uh, it. I mean . . . see what I mean?"

"It will do just fine," said Tar Gibbons.

"What will do just fine?"

"*It* will," he repeated.

"What will?"

"*It.* Refer to me as an it."

"That seems pretty rude," I said nervously.

"Not as rude as calling me a he or a she," it said.

I sighed and turned back to my volcano. I had to think about this for a while.

Before I could get another glob of papier-mâché on the frame, Grakker said, "I've made a decision."

I turned to look at him. I got nervous whenever he said something like that.

"Tomorrow Rod will take us to BKR's house. We should look around inside."

"I can't. I have to go to school."

"No, you have to take us to BKR's house," replied Grakker calmly.

"But if I don't go to school . . ."

Well, you can imagine how that argument

went. If I skipped school, I might get grounded for a while; if I didn't take the aliens to BKR's house, I would be hauled into space to stand trial for obstructing justice.

Grakker might not play fair, but he almost always won his arguments.

Madame Pong fished the little gold transmitter out of her pocket. "I guess we'd better put this back in your ear, Rod," she said.

Flying to my shoulder, she peeled off the patch she had put over the hole Grakker had burned through my earlobe and re-inserted the gold stud. Then she replaced the patch. "Perfect!" she said. "No one will even know it's there."

She had just flown back to my desk when my door swung open and my mother walked in.

The aliens froze.

She walked over to the *Ferkel.* To my horror, she reached down and picked up Grakker.

CHAPTER 9

House Hunting

"WELL," SAID MOM WITH A FROWN, "IS THIS THE toy that caused all the trouble today?"

I looked at her in surprise. "How did you hear about that?"

"Miss Maloney called me. Arnie Markle broke his hand today. His father is threatening a lawsuit."

"Arnie broke his hand trying to punch me!" I cried. "If I hadn't ducked, he might have broken my nose instead of his hand."

My mother sighed. "I know, sweetheart. The thing is, we can't afford any trouble with them. . . ."

I sighed, too. Ever since my father left, we've been tight for money—especially since he doesn't send any support. Sometimes it's hard not to hate him for that.

Mom looked at Grakker. "Maybe if you just gave him this toy—"

"I can't do that!" I shouted.

She blinked, surprised at my reaction.

"It would be wrong," I said desperately. "Like paying them off or something."

To my astonishment, she began to blush. "You're right, honey. I'm sorry; that was a bad idea. But I really don't know what I'm going to do if they actually sue. We just can't afford a lawyer right now."

"Can they really sue us?" I asked. "I didn't do anything wrong. Honest."

"People can sue over almost anything. I don't think the Markles would win, but they can afford it, and we can't. Arnie's dad knows that; this is his way of pushing us around."

"Geez, he's no better than his kid."

"That's the way it goes sometimes," said Mom. She tossed Grakker onto the bed. "Don't leave these lying around, all right?"

She left the room. I could tell that she was trying not to cry. I don't know who I hated more at that moment—Arnie, his father, or my own father, who had left us in a situation where Arnie and his parents could cause us so much trouble.

"Ouch," said Grakker, straightening himself out. "That hurt."

"What am I going to do?" I asked.

"Don't worry about it," he said, dusting himself off and flying back to the desk.

"What do you mean? Why shouldn't I worry about it?"

"You don't have to face Arnie tomorrow. You have to skip school so you can take us to BKR's house. Remember?"

"What a terrific solution," I said with a groan. Flopping onto my bed, I stared at the ceiling, wondering if being taken to Alpha Centauri to stand trial might be the best way out of this mess.

At some point I fell into a sleep that was marked by wild nightmares. Given the state of my life at the moment, it wasn't much different from being awake.

Despite my hopes, my troubles did not magically disappear overnight. On the other hand, they didn't get any bigger, either; they were still two inches tall.

A new thought occurred to me as I was getting dressed.

"You know," I said to Grakker, who was standing on my dresser, examining a monster trading card that looked as if it might be a portrait of one of his relatives, "even if I wanted to skip school, there's no way I could do it."

"Why not?" he asked, setting down the card.

"Well, when I leave the house, my mother will be watching. So I *have* to get on the bus. That takes me straight to school. When I get off at school, there'll be a teacher watching. So just when and how am I supposed to get away to take you to Billy Becker's house?"

"Gracious," said Tar Gibbons, who was climbing out of the ship at that moment. "You don't have much time to yourself. Don't they trust you?"

I thought about pointing out that I had had a lot more time to myself before the *Ferkel* crashed through my window, but I decided against it.

"Do you have any other way of getting to school?" asked Grakker.

I hesitated. If only I could lie!

"Well?" asked Grakker.

I sighed. "I might be able to talk my mother into letting me ride my bike."

We had been talking about me riding to school for some time now. Mom had been resisting because it's so far, but I could tell she was going to relent soon.

"Make it happen," said Grakker.

I sighed again and went to breakfast.

* * *

My mother was looking pretty grim. "I'm sorry about last night, Rod," she said.

I knew at once that I had her. She was in the grip of a guilt attack, and it was going to be easy to talk her into letting me ride the bike.

(Of course, once she found out that I had used the occasion to skip school, it would probably be ten years before she let me ride there on my own again.)

After breakfast I said goodbye to the Things, then climbed onto my bike and pedaled out of the driveway, supposedly heading for school. I had three aliens in my backpack (Tar Gibbons and Phil had again stayed home to work on the ship), a totally different destination in mind, and a load of guilt like you wouldn't believe.

It was a gorgeous spring morning, warm enough that I didn't need a jacket. About a half mile from the house I stopped to ask if the aliens wanted to ride where they could see. Grakker and Snout opted for my front pocket, Madame Pong for my shoulder. I was worried that she might fall off. When she assured me that she could manage it safely, even if she did, I remembered that she was wearing a rocket belt.

The leaves were just budding out, and the air smelled sweet and fresh. (Except for when we passed McGuire's chicken farm; they had just cleaned a winter's worth of manure out of the barns, and the smell was overwhelming.)

"What an aroma!" cried Snout, sounding almost joyous. "It makes me think of home."

I guess life is different everywhere you go.

"Rod," said Madame Pong, speaking directly into my ear, "I know we are making your life difficult. I will try to see that you are rewarded if we survive this mission."

"If?" I yelped. I stopped pedaling, but since we were going downhill, we kept moving.

"I thought we had made it clear that this was very dangerous," she said.

"Then why are you dragging me into this? I'm just a kid."

"Does that exempt you from doing what is necessary?" she asked, sounding puzzled.

"On this planet we save stuff like that for grown-ups. We try to protect kids."

Madame Pong was silent for a moment. Finally she said, "I don't understand. If you try to protect children, why do you let them live where people are shooting at each other all the time?"

I thought about some of the things I had seen on the evening news and decided maybe our society wasn't as serious about protecting kids as it likes to pretend—which left me with nothing to say to Madame Pong, and no excuse for not going to BKR's house.

I knew where Billy Becker lived because once when several of us had stayed late for a special project, his father had given me a ride home. He had pointed out the house as we drove past it. Remembering that ride now, I shivered. I had been driven home by an interstellar criminal!

The Becker house was on the outskirts of town. That made sense, given the fact that it was a criminal hideout. But it worked for our purposes, too. If the house had been in town, I probably would have been stopped by someone wanting to know why I wasn't in school before I could have gotten anywhere near it. Even out of town, I figured we would have better luck if we waited for the morning traffic to die down. So I pulled off the road and hid in a copse of trees beside a little stream.

I sat down on a rock. Grakker, Madame Pong, and Snout used their rocket belts to float down to the bank of the stream. Grakker began to pace back and forth at the edge of the water, his green brow furrowed in concentration.

"How much longer do you think we need to wait?" he asked after about a minute. He reminded me of the Things, asking "How much farther is it?" when we were in the car.

"Probably another half hour," I said. "By that time most people will have made it to work."

He began to pace again. Suddenly he shouted in surprise as he came face to face with a frog. He pulled out his ray gun, but the frog jumped into the water before he could shoot.

Grakker wrinkled his nose.

I tried not to laugh. "What are you going to do when we get there?" I asked.

"It depends on whether there is anyone inside," said Snout.

"How are you going to know that without going and asking?"

"I'll use certain mental techniques to perform a bioscan. This will tell me if there are any large masses of living matter inside. If BKR has left the house for some reason—for example, if he has a job to help maintain his disguise—we can just go inside."

"Don't we have to have a search warrant or something? We have laws against breaking into people's houses, you know. Even criminals' houses."

"BKR is not a citizen of your planet and therefore is not subject to your law," said Grakker.

I wasn't sure that covered the situation, but not being a lawyer, I didn't figure I could argue the matter. So I changed the subject. "What about Mrs. Becker?"

"If she is home, you will talk to her in order to distract her while we slip inside."

"Talk to her about what?"

"Make something up," snapped Grakker.

"I can't! I don't tell lies."

"Then think of something true."

That was a lot of help.

In the end I didn't have to worry about it. Snout's "bioscan" showed no one home.

"Good," said Grakker. "We can all go in."

"*All* of us?"

"That's what I said."

I rode my bike up to the Beckers' front door. Being out of town, there were not a lot of other houses around—just three, in fact, from which we could be seen at all. Snout did another bioscan, checking on the neighbors. Two of the houses were empty. Taking a chance that no one was watching from the third, we rode around back so I could hide the bike. The yard was neat and trim.

Snout took out another device and used it to do a techscan. This was a lot like the bioscan, only now he was looking for any kind of device that would sound an alert if someone entered the house. Any doubts I had about whether there was really an alien in residence here faded when Snout announced that he had found *four* monitoring systems. I might have been able to convince myself that one system was a burglar alarm. Rare, but not impossible. But no one around here has *four* burglar alarms.

After a few minutes of fiddling with the tech-scan control box, Snout said "I have disabled the systems. It is now safe to enter the building."

The aliens directed me to carry them to the back door. I held out my hand like a platform so Snout could stand on it. He took yet another device from his cloak and did something to the lock.

The doorknob turned by itself. The door swung open.

With the aliens riding on my shoulder, I entered BKR's lair. I moved slowly, carefully, expecting something to spring out at me at any second. But the house was almost disappointingly normal. Normal kitchen, normal bathroom, normal living room.

It wasn't until Grakker told me to open the hall closet that I began to scream.

CHAPTER 10

The Real Enemy

HANGING IN THE CLOSET, STARING AT US WITH sightless eyes, were Mr. and Mrs. Becker. "Oh, my god!" I cried. "He killed them. Billy Becker killed his parents!"

"Don't be silly," said Grakker. "Those aren't real people."

"They sure look real!" I said, backing away from the closet.

"They're just androids," said Madame Pong soothingly. She was clinging to my ear so that my violent trembling wouldn't throw her to the floor. "At least, you would call them androids at this stage of your planet's development. The technology is actually a little more advanced than that. But the idea is close enough."

"But that's Mr. Becker! I've met him before."

"No, that is an android that has been out in public using the name Mr. Becker."

"Why would BKR have an android of himself?" I said. "I don't get it."

"I think I do," said Snout. "We've been on the wrong path all this time. Mr. Becker is not our quarry. His *son* is!"

"You mean Billy Becker is an alien criminal?" I cried.

"That would seem to be the logical conclusion," said Madame Pong.

Can you believe it? My archenemy, the rotten lying little creep, was no mere kid. He was a

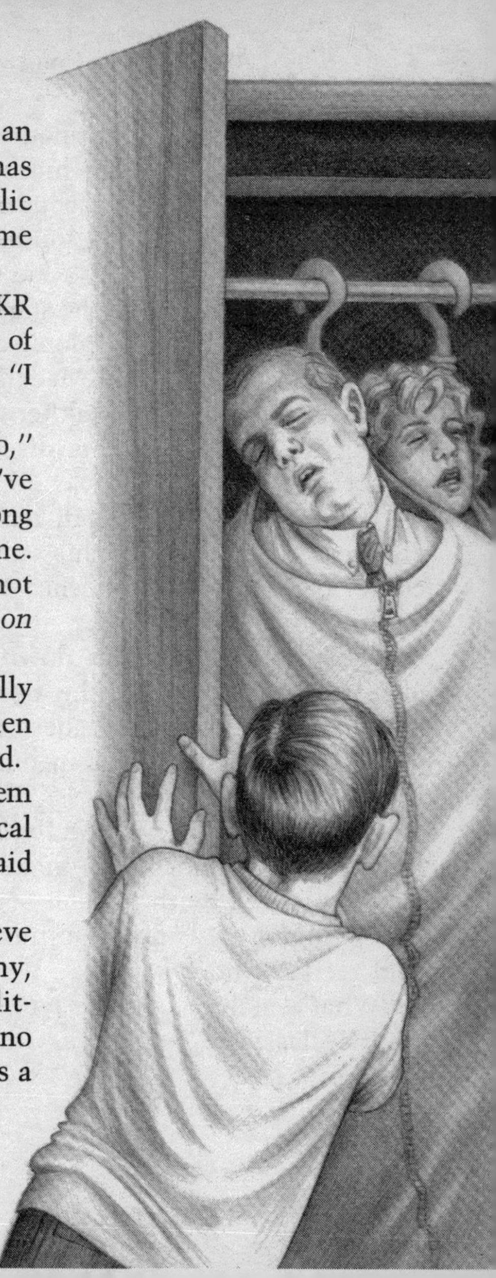

fugitive mastermind from another planet, wanted across the galaxy for his hideous crimes. That should tell you something about *my* life. Most kids get bullied at some point or another. But how many sixth graders get bullied by a kid who turns out to be a criminal genius from the stars in disguise?

"But why?" I asked. "I don't get it."

"I have a theory," said Madame Pong.

"Let's hear it," said Grakker gruffly. I got the feeling he didn't like this discovery any more than I did.

"Well, as near as we can make out, children are close to invisible in this culture. If BKR had come to Earth and established himself as a rich adult with a lot of power, it would have been easy for us to track him down. But simply by appearing to be a child, he was more likely to stay undetected. I would guess that he has been doing this over and over in different places for the last twelve years."

Snout put one of his spindly fingers beside his long nose and said, "That makes sense. It could also have to do with his stat—"

"Divulging classified information is a crime," said Grakker fiercely.

"What was he going to say?" I cried.

"It's classified," repeated Grakker. "We can't tell you."

"Look, if you can drag me away from school to help you with this mission, I think the least you can do is take me into your confidence. What was he going to say?"

Grakker folded his arms, shook his green gorilla head from side to side, and said, "Classified is classified."

"All right, have it your way," I snapped. "We don't have time to argue. We have to get out of here."

"Why?" asked Madame Pong.

"What if Billy . . . er, BKR . . . *whoever!* . . . comes back? We don't want him to catch us here!"

"He'll be in school all day, won't he?" said Grakker.

"I suppose so," I said uneasily.

"Then we must take advantage of this time to examine the house. We may find information that will be useful in capturing him, or that can be used against him when he goes on trial again."

"I thought he was already convicted," I said.

"He is," said Madame Pong. "Grakker would like to go for the maximum punishment."

"What's that?" I asked.

"We make him stay on Earth," said Snout.

"What?"

"Just joking, just joking," he said, tweaking

the end of his nose so that it bounced up and down.

Aliens. Who can figure their sense of humor?

After half an hour of carrying the aliens around, I returned to the living room. Sitting on the floor, I put the aliens on the coffee table so we could look at each other as we talked. The first thing I said was, "This place is so normal it's almost suspicious."

"What do you mean?" asked Madame Pong.

"It's like a magazine version of a real home," I explained. "Too neat and perfect to be real. Almost everyone has some little quirks that make them interesting. You know—they make pot holders out of roadkill, or decorate lampshades with pictures of Elvis, or something. At least, that was what my dad used to say."

I paused as a stab of pain shot through my heart. I tried to let the moment go by, but it was as if something had been let loose in the room.

"Where is your father, Rod?" asked Madame Pong.

"That's classified information," I snapped, sounding ruder than I intended.

She nodded and didn't pursue the question, which I appreciated. Grakker looked puzzled, as if he didn't understand what was going on, but Snout looked away, and his nose drooped.

"Well, we must be missing something," said Madame Pong. "BKR would not be here without items he could use in case of emergency. They must be hidden somewhere."

"A cross-dimensional closet?" suggested Snout.

"What's that?" I asked.

"A storage device," said Grakker. "It's an opening into another dimension, lined with strong, stretchable material that can expand with the amount of stuff you put in it."

"Sort of an unbreakable, interdimensional balloon," added Snout.

"I could use one of those," I said. My own closet was so full of junk that my mother claimed the door should only be opened by trained professionals.

"They're very handy," agreed Madame Pong. "But also a great luxury. They take an enormous amount of energy to maintain."

"BKR can afford the expense," said Grakker. "He is, after all, fabulously wealthy."

"From stealing stuff?" I asked.

"Oh, he doesn't steal things," said Madame Pong. "He was born rich."

"But I thought he was a criminal?"

"There are far worse crimes than stealing,"

said Grakker darkly. "Anyway, BKR certainly has enough energy credits to maintain a cross-dimensional closet."

"Energy credits?" I asked, trying desperately not to get lost in this conversation.

"Energy is our basic unit of exchange," said Snout.

"Makes more sense than gold," added Grakker with a sneer. "Not much you can do with gold once you've got it."

"I'll do an energy check," said Snout before I could ask any more about their monetary system—which was just as well, I guess, since I didn't want to stay in BKR's house any longer than necessary.

The purple alien removed a small device covered with loops of wire from his cloak. Still standing on the coffee table, he began to turn in a small circle. He was about three quarters of the way around when the device began to beep. "Flibbing!" he exclaimed (which I decided must be like shouting "Bingo!" or "Eureka!" in our language). "Take us that way, Rod!"

I extended my arm so the three of them could climb onto my shoulder, then began to walk in the direction Snout had indicated. He kept adjusting his little machine as I walked, sending me right or left as if we were playing a game of "Hot and Cold."

We stopped in front of the TV.

"Here?" I asked.

"By all appearances," said Snout. "Set us on top of it, please."

I did as he asked.

"Wait a minute while I make an adjustment," he said, tinkering with the box he had been holding. "All right, now run this around the edge of the screen."

I took the box from his hands; it was no bigger than a blueberry. Holding it delicately between my fingertips, I did as he had directed.

"Good. Now see if you can pry off the screen."

I put the little box on top of the television, then hooked my fingernails over the edge of the glass. It tipped forward so easily it caught me off guard. I tried to catch it, but it slipped through my fingers and fell to the floor. (Rod the Clod strikes again!) To my relief, it didn't break. Then I realized it probably wasn't actually glass, but some alien material that wouldn't break even if a rhino started tap dancing on it.

"Excellent!" said Grakker. "Let's see what he has in there. Shoulder, please."

I put my hand on the top of the TV and let them walk onto my shoulder. When all three of them were safely in place, I bent forward and put my head through the hole. I felt like I was getting a shock from a small battery; not strong enough to really hurt, but definitely weird. I shouted in surprise.

"What's the matter, Rod?" asked Madame Pong.

"It tingles!"

"Of course it tingles," said Grakker impatiently. "Your head is in one dimension while the rest of your body is in another."

"Is that dangerous?" I asked. "What about my blood? Is it flowing in and out of my regular dimension?"

"Probably," said Snout. "It's very profound, when you think about it. Almost metaphysical."

"Can we skip the philosophy and get this over with?" I asked. "I don't know how much more of this I can take."

"Hold on while I get some light here," said Grakker.

So there I was, my rear end waving around in an alien criminal's living room, my head in another dimension, when a familiar voice cried, "Why, it's Rod Allbright! I'd know that pudgy butt anywhere!"

Billy was home!

I tried to back out of the TV, but before I could get started, someone give me a solid push. I hurtled through the television, out of this world and into the cross-dimensional closet.

CHAPTER 11

The Storage Dimension

BEFORE I COULD SORT MYSELF OUT FROM THE PILES of stuff surrounding me, I heard a click, followed by a laugh.

The click, it turned out, was made by BKR snapping the television screen back in place.

The laugh came from BKR—alias Billy Becker—who was pressing his face against the screen and staring in at us. As I watched, he pushed his face closer and closer, flattening his features against the surface. Soon his nose was spreading out like a blob of melting ice cream. But he kept pressing until his smile had smooshed from one side of the screen to the other, and his eyes looked like a pair of fried eggs with blue yolks.

"Stop!" I cried. "It's disgusting."

BKR giggled—a wild, high-pitched sound that sent a chill down my spine. Then he began to peel his face away from the screen. That's when I realized it was a mask—a Billy Becker mask that had been smushed across the screen.

As he pulled the mask away, I could see the real face of BKR, the alien criminal my tiny companions had crossed a galaxy to capture. His skin was blue. He had orange spikes instead of hair. Other than that, he looked a lot like Shirley Temple.

"What a nice surprise," he said, leering in at us. "That *is* Captain Grakker you've got with you, isn't it, Rod? I thought I recognized him when that idiot Arnie pulled him out of your backpack yesterday."

"Let the boy go, BKR!" shouted Grakker. "He is of no concern to you."

I glanced at Grakker in surprise; it was the first time he had given any indication he cared what happened to me.

BKR snorted. "What does it matter whether he's of any concern to me? I have him, and that's enough."

Of all the things I had experienced so far, I think the coldness in BKR's voice was the most frightening yet.

"No," he continued, "the real concern is, what

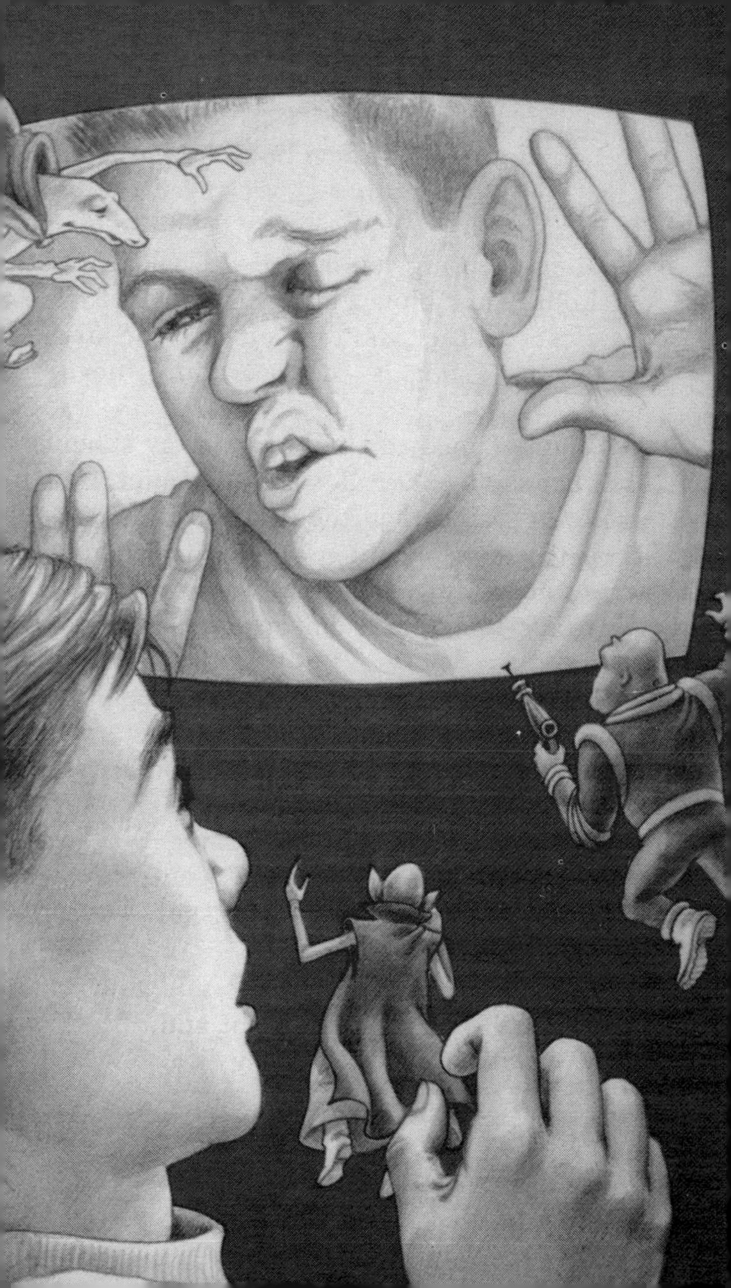

am I going to do with you now? I don't want to leave you alone in my closet—I've got things stored there that might actually be of use to you. But should I bring you out here to take care of? Or should I just blow a hole through the back of the closet and let you drift off into the storage dimension? *That* is the decision I have to make."

Madame Pong had climbed onto my shoulder. I felt her shudder at BKR's last suggestion, which was even scarier than the coldness in his voice. If what he was planning was that frightening to her, I knew *I* sure didn't want to experience it.

"What's the storage dimension like?" I whispered.

"An interplanetary junkyard," she replied, her voice equally soft.

I thought of the junkyard on the other side of Seldom Seen. It was pretty interesting.

"You can find almost anything you want there," added Snout. "Only there's no air in most of it, so we'd probably be dead before we came across anything useful."

"You're awfully calm about this," I whispered.

He bent his nose to the right and said, "I've never improved a situation by worrying about it."

Not having Snout's philosophical training, my own level of fear was quickly building toward pure panic.

The confrontation with BKR was not improved by Grakker shouting, "This is Captain Grakker speaking. Surrender now, or face justice at the hands of the Galactic Patrol."

Madame Pong sighed.

BKR laughed hysterically. "Well, I've made up my mind," he said. "Enjoy the storage dimension, everyone!"

"BKR, stop!" cried Madame Pong.

He ignored her. Holding up what looked like a standard television remote control, he put his finger directly over a button. Smiling in at us, he said, "Bye-bye, boys and girls!"

Before he could lower his finger and send us into the storage dimension, the good ship *Ferkel* zoomed into the room and smacked against his head.

BKR screamed with rage as he fell out of sight.

The *Ferkel* circled the room, then stopped in front of the TV. Hovering in midair, it aimed a purple ray at the screen holding us in the storage dimension. It shimmered and began to melt. But before the *Ferkel* could finish the job, a blue hand reached up and swatted it sideways.

"Quick, Rod!" cried Madame Pong. "Push on the barrier!"

I hesitated. If it was *melting* it would probably be hot enough to burn my hands off.

"Hurry!" cried Grakker. "It's our only hope."

Well, having no hands was better than being totally dead. I lunged forward. To my surprise, the screen wasn't hot at all. It popped out, and I burst through the front of the TV like some full-size jack-in-the-box.

"Good work, Rod!" cried Grakker, zooming over me with his flying pack.

I didn't have time to appreciate the compliment. I had stumbled over the edge of the opening and landed on top of BKR. He looked as if he was interested in making sure I never did anything like that again as long as I lived—mostly by making how long I lived really, really short. Grabbing my skull between his hands, which were astonishingly strong, he began to squeeze.

"I don't have any bugs, Rod!" he yelled. "So why don't I just squish your head instead?"

The pain was incredible. "Stop!" I screamed. "Stop!"

"Unhand that earthling!" roared Grakker, flying overhead and zapping Billy with his ray gun.

"Ow!" cried Billy. He slapped his right hand to

the side of his head where the tiny ray of light had struck him.

It's hard to squeeze something *between* your hands when only one of them is in place. I took the chance to roll out of his grip. Billy bellowed with rage. But before he could grab me, the *Ferkel* sailed in front of him. To my astonishment, an orange ray came out of the bottom and sucked Grakker into the ship. Suddenly I realized that Madame Pong and Snout were nowhere to be seen. Had the ship pulled them in as well?

I feared that they would abandon me in the hands of Billy Becker. That wasn't fair, I now realize. The aliens considered me one of them and were planning to take care of me. Which is why the ship flew over and pointed the ray at me. Only now it was purple instead of orange. I couldn't figure out what they were up to. Were they going to use the tractor beam to pick me up and then fly out of there?

Suddenly I noticed that the room was getting bigger. The chairs seemed to be growing, the walls getting farther away, the ceiling getting higher.

The *Ferkel* was growing, too.

That was when I realized nothing was growing. *I* was getting smaller . . . and smaller . . . and smaller . . . until I was about two inches high.

Before I could figure out what it felt like to be only two inches high, I heard Billy Becker cry, "A bug! I *hate* bugs. It's squishing time!"

It wasn't until I saw his giant hand hurtling toward my head that I realized *I* was the bug he was shouting about.

CHAPTER 12

A Small Problem

"BILLY!" I SCREAMED. "DON'T! IT'S ME, ROD!"

Which shows you how addled I was at that point. To begin with, despite everything that had happened, I was still thinking of BKR as Billy Becker rather than as a desperate interstellar criminal. For an instant I even thought he actually believed I was a bug.

Then I realized it was just his sick sense of humor in operation.

It's amazing how much can go through your head when you see death hurtling at you.

Billy's hand was inches from my head, a microsecond from turning me into a grease spot on the rug, when he screamed and twisted sideways.

The *Ferkel* had struck again!

"Damn you, Grakker!" cried Billy. He was now

lying on the floor and clutching his hand. I figured this wouldn't last. He would be on his feet soon. I wanted to be far away from him by the time he was.

If you've ever tried to catch a mouse or a cockroach, you know that tiny things can move pretty fast. I proved it now by moving faster than I had thought possible. Soon I was going so fast that I started to fly, which has been one of my favorite fantasies for as long as I can remember.

It didn't take long to realize I wasn't flying because I was running too fast; I was flying because the ship had caught me in the orange beam it had used to suck up Grakker and the others. When I was about two feet above the floor, BKR roared and lunged at me. I tried to twist away, but the ray had me in its grip. I couldn't move.

Fortunately, the ray was faster than Billy. He flashed underneath me as I was lifted into the ship.

"Get us out of here, Phil!" I heard Grakker command as the doors slid shut beneath me. I felt the ship accelerate. Then, suddenly, we came to a full stop.

"He's got us!" cried Madame Pong.

"Full reverse blasters!" ordered Grakker.

"Aye, aye, Captain!" said a voice that I recognized as belonging to the potted plant.

A roar. A scream from BKR. The ship shot forward, and we hurtled through a window without breaking it, mostly because it had already been broken when the *Ferkel* flew in.

When we were free of BKR's house, Madame Pong came to stand beside me. I *felt* like she had gotten taller, even though I knew the opposite was true. The fact that the ship's furniture was the right size added to the illusion; after all, it was easier to believe that the furniture was full-size than to believe that at that moment I could fit inside my mother's coffee cup!

"Are you all right, Rod?" Madame Pong asked, a worried look creasing her yellow face.

"I'm not sure. . . ."

"He's probably in shock," said Tar Gibbons. The four-legged alien walked over, put an orangish hand on my forehead, and stared at me with goggley eyes. My first thought was that this was no way to make me feel better. Then, oddly, I *did* start to feel better.

"Are you casting a spell on me?" I cried, flinching away from its hand.

"Don't be silly. I'm simply easing some of your tension."

"How?"

Madame Pong shook her head. "Don't ask. It's

even more complicated than trying to explain how gender works on Tar Gibbons's planet."

"T-chah, Madame," said Tar Gibbons. "It's not complicated at all. I'm working at the subatomic level to alter the electron flow affecting young Rod Allbright's endocrine system and causing him feelings of fear. Nothing mystic about it—it's basic Warrior Science."

Suddenly a furry creature went scurrying past me. Except for the fact that it was blue, it looked like a cross between a cat and a monkey.

"What was *that?*" I cried.

"Plink," said Madame Pong.

I wasn't sure if the word was the name of the creature or simply a flaw in her language program. "Plink?" I asked.

"He's Phil's assistant."

"*Symbiote* would be a better word," said Tar Gibbons, "since the two species co-evolved." Turning to me, it added, "Plink is the moving half of the partnership. He runs and fetches

for Phil. In return, he gets to eat any leaves, branches, and nuts that Phil is done with."

Tar Gibbons must have seen the look on my face, because its eyes got bigger and it added, "Biology is strange and wonderful, and not subject to moral judgment, Young Rod Allbright."

Before I could answer, or ask the Tar why it kept calling me "Young Rod Allbright," Plink went scooting back in the other direction, carrying something that looked like the interstellar version of a monkey wrench. The little animal zipped through a door into what I took to be the cabin of the ship and stopped. I couldn't see Phil, but I did see a long green tendril unroll and lift the wrench out of Plink's paws.

"Would you like a tour of the ship?" asked Madame Pong.

"Yes, please," I said. "But what about BKR?"

"He'll be after us soon, I imagine. But there's not much I can do about it. That's Grakker's job. I am the Diplomatic Officer for the ship, and right now I am offering my services."

"But shouldn't we do *something?*"

"Action taken without thought is like giving an egg a navel," said Tar Gibbons, blinking and waving its long neck.

"Is that supposed to mean something?" I asked.

"It should—unless this dingbutted language

program is malfunctioning again." It turned to Madame Pong and said in a cranky voice, "Can't you do something about the quality of the equipment they give us?"

Putting her hands together, she made one of her little bows. "I shall do my best," she said quietly. Walking around behind him, she gave him a solid whack at the back of his head. "There," she said. "That ought to take care of it for the time being."

"Thank you," said the Tar.

Reaching for my hand, Madame Pong said, "Come, Rod. Let me show you the ship."

Now that I was two inches tall, the *Ferkel* was in perfect proportion to me. Except in one case, each of the aliens had his, her, or its own room. Madame Pong didn't show me all of them, but she did open the door to her own room, which was slightly larger than my own bedroom. Sheets of gauzy fabric, in colors ranging from pale yellow to a purple so deep it was almost black, hung from her ceiling, making the room look as if it were filled with a rainbow mist.

"Walk in," she said, gesturing toward the door.

The fabric trailed over my skin as I entered. It tingled and tickled, as if it had the tiniest electric current running through it.

"This feels weird!" I cried.

She smiled, made one of her tiny bows, and said simply, "I am happy in this room."

Next she showed me Phil's room, which, not surprisingly, was something like a jungle. "Phil is on a quest for his roots," said Madame Pong in a hushed voice. "This is a holy endeavor, and we are privileged to have him with us. When he is not working, he often comes here to be alone, and to turn over a new leaf."

I started to laugh, then realized that I had no idea whether she was joking or serious. Since I was a guest and didn't want to offend her, I didn't ask. I just put my hands together and made a tiny bow, which seemed to please her.

"Because of his vows, Phil considers his room to be open to all when he is not inside it himself. The room shared by Grakker and Snout is private. However, if Tar Gibbons has no objections, we can see its personal space."

"That is amazingly all right," said Tar Gibbons, stretching its neck so that its head came over my shoulder, startling me a little.

Tar Gibbons's room was actually a pond, with a large rock in the center. A thick mist hovered in the room, and little squeaking sounds filled the air.

"Lovely, isn't it?" asked Tar Gibbons, who stood next to me at the door. Before I could answer, a small winged thing flew past. Almost faster than I could see, a hand shot forward. Grabbing the winged thing out of the air, Tar Gibbons popped the creature into its mouth. "I grow my own snacks," it said cheerfully, crunching as it spoke.

"How . . . ecological," I replied.

Madame Pong was showing me the recreation room, which had wall-size viewing screens and shape-shifting furniture, when Grakker's voice filled the air. "All crew members to the main deck at once. That includes the earthling deputy. Emergency Alert. I repeat: Emergency Alert!"

"Oh, dear," said Madame Pong. "Come along, Rod."

I followed the two aliens to an elevator, which was really just a tube. The three of us crowded in, the door closed, I heard a *whoosh,* and the next thing I knew we were in the ship's control room.

Grakker was sitting at a console filled with lights, buttons, balls, and levers, all of them marked with labels (at least, I assume they were labels) written in a language that didn't look like anything else I had ever seen. Snout stood at his shoulder, eyes closed, as if concentrating on the infinite. Across the room Phil floated in front of a wall full of mechanical devices. The light from his main blossom was focused on a row of switches, and his leaves were waving in an agitated fashion as he used several tendrils to manipulate the controls.

"What is it, Grakker?" asked Madame Pong as we entered the room.

It was Snout who answered. His voice was solemn. "I have been running some calculations, and I have anticipated BKR's next move."

"And it is . . . ?" prompted Tar Gibbons.

"He will kidnap someone from Rod's family."

"This is terrible!" I cried. "We have to stop him!"

"It's worse than you can imagine," whispered Madame Pong. Glancing at her, I was horrified to see that she had actually turned white.

"What do you mean, it's worse than I can imagine? What could be worse than BKR kidnapping someone from my family?"

Tar Gibbons's eyes had sunk back into its head. The pupils were like tiny points of blackness. "We haven't yet told you the nature of BKR's crime."

CHAPTER 13

A Big Problem

"WELL, WHAT IS IT?" I CRIED. "WHAT IS HIS crime?"

"Cruelty," whispered Snout.

I felt my stomach tighten. "Cruelty?" I asked, wondering if I had heard right.

"In the civilized galaxy, cruelty is the greatest of all crimes," said Madame Pong. "Of course, life always involves some suffering, and there are times when painful things must be done for life to continue. But an intelligent being who takes pleasure in causing pain to others—well, such a being is considered dangerously bent."

"You must understand," said Tar Gibbons, "that empathy is the heart of civilization."

"Empathy?"

"The ability to understand what another feels,"

said Snout. "It is the trait that lifts us above the animals."

"Speak for yourself," burped Phil.

"You know what I mean," said Snout smoothly. "An intelligent being who lacks empathy is a threat to the social order. Not caring what pain it causes, it may do damage beyond estimation. Causing needless suffering is a sickness, and those who do so are forever outside our law."

I had a sudden, sinking feeling that I knew why Earth had not yet been invited to join the League of Worlds. If you've watched the evening news more than once, I'm sure I don't have to explain.

"Just how cruel *is* this guy?" I asked, hoping that if cruelty was a crime, squashing bugs against the heads of innocent kids might be enough to get BKR in the kind of trouble that would send the Galactic Patrol across the galaxy to capture him.

"Millions have wept," murmured Madame Pong.

That didn't sound good. "But what has he *done?*" I persisted.

"That is classified information!" snapped Grakker, giving me a sudden desire to hit him on the head.

"Rod, if he kidnaps someone from your family,

you can be sure that at least part of his motive will be to cause *you* pain and suffering," said Tar Gibbons.

"But what will he do to them?" I persisted.

"Nothing, if we can stop him in time," said Snout. "Where are your mother and siblings now?"

"They should be at home."

"Oh, dear," said Madame Pong.

I think that simple phrase was the most frightening thing I had heard yet.

"Back to the Allbright residence!" shouted Grakker.

"Aye, aye, Captain Meathead," burped Phil.

My stomach lurched as the ship made a sharp turn and then shot forward. "Hurry," I cried. "Hurry!"

"We're there," said Grakker. "How much faster do you want us to go?"

"We're *there*? But we just started." Then I blushed. We were in a spaceship. The three miles from the Becker house to my house might have taken a quarter of an hour on my bike, but that was no reason to expect the same of the good ship *Ferkel*.

"Snout!" called Grakker. "Do a bioscan. See if you can detect any life-forms in the house—especially those of the Allbright larvae."

Snout closed his eyes. The end of his snout began to quiver, as if he were trying to smell the twins. "I detect one humanoid life-form," he said at last.

"Mom?" I cried.

"No, not your mother. Nor is it BKR. This is someone unfamiliar to me."

I felt a little chill. "Who could it be?" I asked.

"We'll have to go down and find out," said Grakker grimly.

While Phil landed the *Ferkel* in the apple tree behind the house, Grakker handed me a wide belt. "Strap this on," he said.

"What is it?"

"Rocket pack, standard issue, same as I use. Basically an antigravity belt with thrusters for control. Use the buttons on the front to direct yourself."

Madame Pong looked worried. "Grakker, do you think—"

"Madame," he said, holding up a green hand, "this is a captain's decision. Rod must accompany us, and the belt is the only efficient way for him to do so."

She closed her eyes and nodded her head. Then she turned to me and said, "Be careful, young one."

I hadn't really been worried until she did that. Now I felt nervous indeed. "Be careful of what?" I asked.

"Of flying. Of surprises. Of cruelty. My thoughts will be with you."

"Just your thoughts? Aren't you coming along?"

"This is a scouting mission," said Grakker. "I need you because you know the territory. Tar Gibbons will accompany us in case we need his fighting skills. Snout, please perform a training transfer."

Before I could ask what a "training transfer" was, Snout had placed his long fingers at the sides of my head. "Close your eyes, Rod," he whispered, standing as close as he could without jamming his long face into mine. "And whatever you do, don't move!"

I did as he asked. He began to hum. Suddenly my mind was filled with an image of the control panel at the front of the rocket belt.

"How did you do that?" I cried, pulling away from him.

Instead of answering, he screamed and fell to the floor.

"What happened?" I cried. "What is it?"

"He told you not to move!" snapped Grakker, kneeling beside the fallen alien. With a gentleness that surprised me, he lifted Snout's head into his lap.

"But he startled me," I said weakly.

"Warrior mind must deal with surprise more fluidly," said Tar Gibbons, sticking its head over my shoulder.

Snout had his hands crossed over his eyes. He was moaning softly.

"Your sudden move broke the connection that poor Snout had established," explained Madame Pong. "That breaking must be done slowly and gently. Otherwise much pain can ensue."

I felt terrible. "I'm sorry," I said, kneeling beside Snout and touching his hand. His long fingers closed over mine. The skin felt like fine leather stretched over sticks.

"No matter," he muttered, "no matter. See to the children."

"Come, earthling," said Grakker, getting to his feet. "Madame Pong will take my friend to the healing table. We must move on to the task at hand."

To my surprise, I saw a tear trickle down his green cheek. It left a glistening trail in its wake.

"I'm sorry," I said again, feeling helpless.

Snout tightened his grip on my hand. "You made a mistake. Forgiveness is granted. The pain will pass. It is not the pain of cruelty. Forget me. Save the children!"

I stood. Grakker and Tar Gibbons led me to an exit in the side of the ship. The door opened. I looked down—and nearly fainted. I had climbed this old tree plenty of times, and I knew it well. I had often stood on this very branch. It was about twelve feet above the ground. But now that I was only two inches high—about a thirtieth of my normal height—I felt as if I was standing at the edge of a skyscraper.

"Go ahead," said Grakker. "Jump!"

I didn't move.

"Jump, or I'll have to push you. We have no time to waste."

"Grakker, wait!" said Tar Gibbons. "We can't be sure that the training transfer was effective, especially since . . ."

The warning came too late. Grakker had already given me a push. A small push, to be sure; just enough to knock me off the branch.

Screaming, I hurtled toward the ground so far below.

CHAPTER 14

Bonehead

I HAD ONLY FALLEN A COUPLE OF FEET (THOUGH IT seemed as if I had gone much farther) when a strange feeling forced me to grab my belt buckle. Somehow I knew I was supposed to do something with it. The problem was, I wasn't sure *what.*

I started poking and pushing frantically at the buckle as I flashed past the white blossoms that covered the tree.

Suddenly Tar Gibbons was next to me. "The center button!" it cried, stretching its long neck forward so that its face was close to mine. *"Push the center button!"*

Something clicked in my brain, and instantly my fingers found the button. I pushed it, and my fall began to slow. Soon I hung suspended about two feet above the ground—though at my size even two feet looked like a long way down.

Then, as if a computer program had been loaded into my brain, I knew how to make the belt lift me again. Twisting a pair of buttons, I floated up to join Tar Gibbons, who was hovering a foot or so above me. It smiled, and together we flew back to where Grakker was waiting, about halfway between the ship and the low point of my fall.

"What happened?" I asked. "How come I know what to do?"

"Snout implanted the knowledge in your head," said Tar Gibbons. "However, your premature severing of your connection to him hindered your ability to access the information. That was why I had to prompt you. Giving you the first hint should have opened the gateway; I suspect that you now have full access to the information you need to control the belt."

I knew the Tar was right, without knowing how I knew. Twisting the dials, I flew in a circle around them. It was wonderful. Unfortunately, I had no time to enjoy it.

"Okay," I said. "I can handle myself. Now what do we do?"

"We sneak inside to see what we can find out,"

said Grakker. "That's your first job: to tell us the best way in."

I thought for a moment. "We can't count on any of the windows being open—they might be, but it would take us a while to check them out. There's a crack in the cellar door that might work, but we *could* get stuck there. I know! We can go through the pet flap in the kitchen door."

"Pet flap?" asked Tar Gibbons.

"It's a special little door that lets the dog go in and out on his own."

"Very thoughtful," said Tar Gibbons approvingly.

I decided not to tell it that Mom had installed the flap more for *our* convenience than for Bonehead's.

"Lead the way," said Grakker.

Tapping the controls on my flying belt, I zoomed around the corner of the house. I loved the fact that I could use the thing so smoothly, as if I had been flying with it for years. I wondered if Snout could do a training transfer that would teach me how to play soccer without tripping over my feet. That thought flashed in and out of my head. The thought that stayed was the question: *Who's in the house?*

Bonehead's door flap was about six times higher than I was now, and so thick I could barely grip it in my hands. It took all three of us to lift it far enough so that we could slip underneath. Grakker, who was even stronger than he looked, was able to hold it up while Tar Gibbons and I scurried through. Then he joined us.

Someone was sitting at the kitchen table. Before I could see who it was, Bonehead came skidding into the room, barking and growling.

Grakker, Tar Gibbons, and I flew straight up. We landed on top of one of the cupboards. "We can hide here," I said, stepping behind one of Mom's vases, a flowered thing that loomed above me like a monument. Grakker and Tar Gibbons joined me. Bonehead stared up at where we had gone and continued to whine.

"Gracious, dog, whatever is the matter with you?" asked a creaky voice.

My eyes went wide with surprise as I recognized the voice.

Grakker put his face next to my ear. "Who is it?" he whispered.

"Mrs. Nesbitt," I replied. "She's this old lady my mother helps out sometimes. I have no idea what she's doing here."

Just then Little Thing One came running into the kitchen.

"I thought Snout said the twins weren't here,"

I said. I spoke louder than I had intended, which started Bonehead barking again.

"Look again," said Tar Gibbons, stretching its neck over my shoulder. "That is *not* your sister."

The surge of relief I had felt at seeing Little Thing One disappeared as I realized that Tar Gibbons was right. In fact, now that I looked more closely, I was surprised that I had been fooled for even a moment. Whatever had just run into the kitchen wasn't Linda, but some sort of sloppy copy of her.

"Low-grade simulacrum," muttered Grakker. "I wonder why the old woman doesn't realize it."

"Her eyesight is terrible," I replied. (I happened to know this for certain because one of the things my mother sometimes did for Mrs. Nesbitt was read the newspaper to her.)

"We need to find out what she knows," said Tar Gibbons.

Mrs. Nesbitt stood and shuffled over to where Bonehead stood yapping at us. "You just hush!" she said, giving the dog a little slap on the top of his head. "You'll disturb the children."

Bonehead whined and sank back on his haunches, but continued to stare at the top of the cabinet.

"How can we talk to her?" I asked.

"We have to go back to the ship," said Tar Gibbons.

"Huh?"

"Phil can set it up from there. Don't argue, just tell us how to get past the dog. We can't get through that flap while he's sitting there."

"His biscuits are in a box on the shelf," I said. "If we drop one of them on the other side of the room, it should distract him long enough for us to get out."

"Good," said Grakker. "Do it."

"Me?"

"He's less apt to get upset with you than with either of us."

"Less likely to eat you, for that matter," said Tar Gibbons calmly.

I sighed. Touching the front of my belt, I floated from the cabinet down to the shelf. Bonehead started barking again. He didn't stop, even when I disappeared into the box of dog biscuits.

The smell inside the box was overwhelming. The biscuits were as long as I was tall, and I wasn't sure I would be able to lift one. But as soon as I grabbed one, it seemed to become weightless, so I guess the antigravity function of the belt extended to anything I was holding.

I floated out of the box with the dog biscuit. Bonehead's barking got louder than ever.

"What *is* it?" cried Mrs. Nesbitt.

Barking and yelping, Bonehead chased me across the kitchen. I realized that he could swallow me in one bite. I wondered what it would be like to be eaten by my own dog!

Mrs. Nesbitt tried to grab him, and for one horrible moment I was afraid he was going to trip her. Fortunately, he slid around her. Yipping and howling, he followed me—and the dog biscuit—out of the room.

When I got to the dining room, I dropped the biscuit behind a chair, in a spot where Bonehead could get it, but not without a little work. As he

dived for the biscuit, I turned around and flew back to the kitchen, this time skimming along the ceiling, where I knew Mrs. Nesbitt was unlikely to see me.

Tar Gibbons and Grakker were waiting at the pet flap. Seconds later we were outside again.

"All right, that should do it," said Phil a few minutes later. "Give it a try."

We were back in the ship, and the aliens had set up a system to make a phone call into the house—along with an amplifier that would make my voice loud enough for Mrs. Nesbitt to hear me.

A ringing sound came from the wall where Phil did all his work. After the first ring I heard a shriek. It wasn't the phone, it was Plink. The little creature was clinging to Phil's main stem and peeking at me from between two leaves.

Another ring, and then another. Then—"Hello?"

"Hello, this is Rod. Is my mother there?"

I had almost said, "What happened to my mother?" But I realized that would sound suspicious, since supposedly I had no idea that she wasn't there.

"Is that you, Rod? This is Mrs. Nesbitt, dear.

Where are you? Your mother is out looking for you."

"What?"

"Well, the school called and wanted to know where you were. They said you didn't show up this morning. Are you all right, dear? Your mother was awfully worried. Anyway, she asked me to watch the twins while she went to look for you. You know I hate to do that. They make me *so* nervous. But they're behaving quite well, thank goodness."

I felt terrible. Mom must have been worried big time if she asked Mrs. Nesbitt to watch the Things. She was probably driving all over looking for me right now.

"Has anyone else been there this morning?" I asked.

"Why, yes, dear. That nice Billy Becker stopped in a while ago. Shouldn't he be in school, too? And where are you, dear? Your mother is awfully worried."

"Tell her I'm fine."

"Ask her if BKR left a message," whispered Madame Pong.

I nodded.

"Mrs. Nesbitt, did Billy leave a message for me?"

"Now, let me think. Oh, yes—he said to tell you that he would be waiting for you out in Seldom Seen. He said he has something that you would want. What does that mean, Rod? And what is going on, anyway? Your mother is awfully worried, dear. You're not doing anything dangerous, are you?"

The only way to answer that question without lying was to ignore it altogether. "Tell Mom not to worry about me. Tell her I'll be home as soon as I can."

I hung up.

"Where is Seldom Seen?" asked Grakker.

"It's the family name for the place I took you the first day you landed, when you tried to enlarge the ship."

"How does BKR know about it?" asked Snout. He was leaning against the doorframe at the far side of the room.

I was relieved to see him up and around, though that relief was short-lived when Madame Pong exclaimed, "Snout! You should be resting!"

"No time for that," he said, waving his long fingers. "How does BKR know about this place, Rod?"

"I took him there once." I blushed a little. "I was trying to make friends with him. I thought if I made friends with him, maybe I could get him to stop beating me up."

"Nice idea," said Grakker. "Wrong bully. Phil, set course for Seldom Seen."

"But I don't understand," I said. "Why would Billy kidnap the twins and then tell us where he has them? What's the point?"

"The point?" asked Grakker. "It's to get me, of course. He's using your siblings as bait. Naturally, he is also enjoying the fact that it is causing *you* a lot of mental pain. But I'm the one he wants to catch."

"Seldom Seen, straight ahead," burped Phil, surprising me, until I remembered how fast the *Ferkel* could travel. "Uh-oh. Looks like trouble."

"Show us," said Grakker.

Phil flipped a switch. A huge view screen appeared on the wall. It showed the field. When Phil stretched out a tendril and twisted a knob, the image on the screen zoomed in on the center of the field.

BKR stood there, smiling evilly.

Madame Pong gasped. It took me a moment to see what had upset her.

Then I spotted the twins. They were floating about thirty feet above the ground. Beneath them was an open pit with long green flames shooting out of it.

BKR made a gesture, and as if by magic, fiery purple words appeared in the air above him:

GRAKKER—
SURRENDER YOUR SHIP
AND YOUR CREW,
OR ELSE IT'S TIME
FOR A BARBECUE!

CHAPTER 15

Madame Pong Steps In

"ACTIVATE EXTERNAL SPEAKERS AND MICROphones!" commanded Grakker.

"Aye, aye, sir," said Phil. A pair of green tendrils writhed out from among his leaves and threw some switches.

Leaning close to what I took to be a microphone, Grakker snapped, "BKR, release those children immediately!"

BKR waved his hands. The purple words in the air above him shimmered and disappeared. "The children are mine!" he said, his words coming clearly through the speaker system. "Surrender now, or you will be very sorry."

"Would he really hurt them?" I asked. At least I thought I asked it, until I realized my throat was so tight with fear that no sound had come out. I swallowed and tried again. "Would he really hurt them?"

"Of course," said Tar Gibbons.

"Wait! I've got an idea. Why don't we shrink *him?*"

Grakker shook his head. "He will be shielded against that possibility."

"Okay, so we shrink the twins instead and get them away from him."

"Possible, but unlikely," said Snout, hobbling across the room to stand beside me. "We got *you* away from him by shrinking you. BKR is not likely to let that happen twice. While success is not out of the question, odds are high that the attempt will result in injury to the younglings."

"Then what are we going to do?"

Grakker placed his hand over the microphone so that only we could hear him and said, "We're going to surrender."

"We are?" I cried in astonishment.

"We have no choice. Any sign of attack on our part and BKR will drop your siblings into that pit without a second thought. According to Galactic Code, such larvae must be protected."

"But can we count on him to keep his word? Will he really let the twins go if you surrender?"

"It is my duty to negotiate that certainty," said Grakker.

I was somewhat astonished that Grakker was so concerned about the twins' safety. Obviously they belonged to a different legal category than sixth graders like me. Which brought up the next question: "When we surrender, what will BKR do to *us?*"

"Millions have wept," murmured Madame Pong.

Tar Gibbons rested its head on my shoulder and said, "Remember, Young Rod Allbright: All is not lost until all is lost."

"Microphone off!" said Grakker.

"Aye, aye," burped Phil.

Grakker turned and looked each of us full in the eyes. For the second or so that he was looking at me, I saw in his face a kind of sorrow I wouldn't have expected him to be able to feel. It was in that moment that I understood what it meant for him to surrender his ship.

Finally he turned to Snout. The ship's Mental Officer rested one long-fingered hand on Grakker's broad shoulder and said, "My sympathies, my captain."

Grakker nodded gruffly and turned to his control panel. "Microphone on!" he commanded. Then, speaking softly, he said, "BKR! Hear my words. We will surrender once the children are safely on the ground."

"How do I know I can trust you?" asked BKR.

Grakker hesitated. "Spacer's Oath," he said at last.

Madame Pong gasped.

Tar Gibbons stretched its neck to lay its head on my shoulder again. "The captain is bound by that oath in a way that is hard to explain," it whispered. "By law and by training, he cannot break it."

"I understand," I replied, thinking of my mother's chocolate cookies.

"Oath accepted," said BKR. "Here are the terms. I will let the children down and allow them to return home unharmed. In exchange, you will land your ship by that rock." He paused and pointed to a big stone about twenty feet in front of him. "All crew members will then exit and throw down their weapons." He took something from his pocket. "According to my readings, there are six beings on the ship. Make sure you *all* come out!"

Grakker's eyes widened. His nostrils flared, and he began to grind his teeth.

"What's wrong?" I whispered to Tar Gibbons.

Grakker answered the question himself. Placing his hand over the microphone, he said, "The instrument BKR used to determine the population of our ship checks animal life only. I'd bet a Fermian Snibble on it. *He doesn't know Phil is here!* If I hadn't taken a Spacer's Oath, we could bring Plink out with us and leave Phil on the ship."

"What good would that do?" I asked.

"Basic Warrior Science tells us it is always good to have an element of which your enemy is unaware," explained Tar Gibbons. "It may prove worthless; it may save your hide."

Grakker lifted his hand from the microphone. Through clenched teeth he said, "Release the children. When they are out of danger, we will exit."

I turned my attention to the view screen. BKR took something that looked like a TV remote control out of his pocket. He pushed a button, and the flame in the pit disappeared. Another button caused the twins to begin drifting slowly toward the ground. They landed about five feet from the side of the pit.

"Now run home!" said BKR.

"You're a bad person!" shouted Little Thing One. "I hope you poop your pants!" Then she grabbed Eric's hand, and the two of them ran for the edge of the field.

"All right, Grakker," said BKR. "The children are free. I will accept your surrender now."

Before Grakker could move, Madame Pong

stepped over to stand beside him. Slipping one hand over the microphone, she reached up to the back of his head and pulled out the module she had inserted the afternoon the ship crashed in my room.

Snout made a move to stop her, then lowered his hand, as if he thought better of it.

Grakker stood as though frozen.

Removing another module from her pocket, Madame Pong slipped it into Grakker's skull, saying, "I hope this one functions more efficiently than that diplomatic module did."

"What is it?" I asked.

"Docility module," she said as a gentle smile spread over Grakker's face.

He turned to her and said, "Well, the torch has passed. What are you going to do, Madame?"

"I am assuming command of the ship," she replied. Her voice was like steel wrapped in velvet. "Phil, order Plink to exit with Snout. You yourself will stay on board. Be ready for action. The rest of us will exit in a moment. Grakker, tell BKR we're on the way out."

With a dreamy smile Grakker removed his hand from the microphone and said, "We will be exiting the ship momentarily."

"Now turn off the microphone," said Madame Pong.

Grakker nodded and did as she told him.

"I don't understand," I said.

"Captain Grakker is bound by his oath," said Madame Pong. "I, however, am a diplomat. While I am also bound by the oath he has made, the restrictions on my profession are not quite so strict. After all, I make my living telling little white lies. BKR wanted six of us to exit, and six is what he'll get."

"He also said he wanted *all* of us to exit," said Grakker. He was leaning against the control panel with a contented look on his face.

I had been thinking the same thing but hadn't dared to say it.

"He's getting half of what he asked for," said Madame Pong. "That's a better deal than most of us get out of life."

We left the ship in single file. BKR (who looked like a ten-story building from my current size) stared down at us. He looked extra hard at Plink, who was riding on Snout's shoulder, but didn't say anything. Grakker's guess had been right: Our enemy didn't realize we still had one crew member on board the *Ferkel.*

"All right, climb in here," said BKR, pointing to a plastic box at his feet. It took me a moment to recognize it: It was Little Thing One's lunch box, something she had made Mom buy her after she saw me carrying my own lunch box to school a couple of times a week. Now it looked like a small house. (Well, a small yellow house with Smurfs all over it.)

Walking over to the box, I jumped up and grabbed the edge. With a boost from Grakker, I managed to climb in. Tumbling over the side, I landed in a pile of stale food and broken toys that Linda had been collecting.

The other aliens soon joined me. I was still trying to untangle myself from the hair of a severed Barbie-doll head when BKR slammed down the lid.

Until that moment I had never considered how dark it would be inside a lunch box. We might as well have been in a coal bin at midnight—until two circles of light suddenly appeared.

"What's that?" I cried. I was so startled that I stepped backward. Naturally, I tripped over a piece of the debris littering the slick floor of the lunch box. "Ow!" I said as I landed on something sharp.

"Are you all right, Rod?" asked Madame Pong.

"I'm fine, I just fell on something. But what's making those lights?"

"It's me!" said Tar Gibbons. The lights went out, then came back on, and I realized it was a result of the Tar blinking. The light was coming from its eyes!

Aliens.

"What the heck is this thing, anyway?" I asked, picking up the object that had poked me in the side when I fell.

I didn't really expect an answer; it was just one of those things you say. So I was startled when Tar Gibbons shouted, "Flibbix be honored, it's a Warrior Miracle!"

CHAPTER 16

The Next Module

"WHAT IS IT?" I ASKED AGAIN AS THE OTHER ALIENS crowded around us.

Grakker yawned. "Nothing much," he said, "just the missing F/D Gizmo."

"Isn't that what you need to enlarge the ship?" I cried.

"Oh, yes," he replied. "Not having it has caused us a great deal of trouble."

I wondered why Grakker was so calm about this, until I remembered that he still had the "docility module" in his head.

"What's it doing in here?" I asked.

Snout took the F/D Gizmo from my hands. "I suspect it was torn from the ship when we crashed through your window. Odds are, one of your siblings found it and thought it was a toy."

So Little Thing One had been carrying around the missing piece in her lunch box full of toys all this time! It just goes to show: You shouldn't ignore kids.

"All we have to do to enlarge the *Ferkel*—and ourselves—is mount that in the proper slot on the outside of the ship," explained Tar Gibbons.

"Great," I replied. "Only we're locked inside a lunch box, and the *Ferkel* is out there. So how are we going to get it onto the ship?"

"Planjite-fribble wasn't smelled with a single sniff," said Tar Gibbons, nodding the way it did whenever it had said something it considered to be particularly wise.

"What does that mean?" I asked.

"It means discovering the F/D Gizmo is a starting point," said Madame Pong. "What we have to do next is find a way to get one or more of us out of this prison so we can—"

Her words were interrupted by what felt like an earthquake. The floor became the wall as we tumbled sideways, landing in a jumbled heap of Legos, doll parts, and stale crackers. It took me a moment to realize what had happened. It was simple, really: BKR had picked up the box.

Suddenly the whole box began to shake. Plink screeched and grabbed me around the neck as we bounced up and down, then began slamming from side to side. Bits of toys—not to mention other aliens—were flying all around me. I felt as if I was trapped in a popcorn popper.

"What's going on?" I cried. "What is he doing?"

"Shaking us!" shouted Tar Gibbons as it bounced past me.

"But why?" I cried as a plastic dinosaur whizzed past my head.

"Because he wants to," said Grakker. "He probably thinks it's funny."

"Millions have wept," said Madame Pong.

"Make that a million and one!" I shouted.

Suddenly the shaking stopped. Once more the six of us lay in a heap at the current bottom of the box, which at the moment happened to be the side with the hinges. Plink clung to my neck and whimpered pitifully.

A crack of light appeared at the top of the box.

"Having fun?" asked BKR. Then he laughed—that same spine-chilling laugh I had heard one other time—and slammed the lid shut again.

A half an hour later we were back in BKR's house. We were still locked in Thing One's lunch box. The only reason we knew where we were was that Madame Pong had a radio connection to Phil, and he was able to see what was going on through the view screens of the *Ferkel.* He reported to Madame Pong, who repeated it to us word for word:

"The enemy is carrying your prison in his right hand. Now he is tucking the *Ferkel* under his left arm and heading back toward the swamp. Aha! He has a small flying vehicle hidden here. He is stowing the *Ferkel* and the box in the back of his flying machine. Vision blocked for now—more reports later."

During the silence that followed, we tucked the F/D Gizmo into my backpack, on the theory that it would be just as well to have it hidden in case we ever did manage to get out of our plastic prison. As I was fastening the strap that holds the pack shut, Madame Pong closed her eyes—a sign that she was getting a message from Phil—and said, "We are back at the Becker house. BKR has removed us from his flying machine. He is carrying us into the room where we had our last confrontation with him. He's looking around, as if trying to find something. Now he is leaving the room."

"Good," said Tar Gibbons. "This is our chance to get out of here."

"Any suggestions on how we do that?" I asked.

"Yes, I have a simple suggestion. And you know what it is, don't you Madame Pong?"

Madame Pong looked at Tar Gibbons in horror. "You don't mean . . ."

"Madame, Warrior Science tells us that when there is no other choice, we make the choice we must."

"While the thought fills me with fear and loathing, I have to say that I believe the Tar is right," said Snout.

All of them turned toward Grakker. "Hey, whatever you guys want is fine with me," he said, spreading his hands and smiling.

"What are you talking about?" I cried.

Madame Pong rummaged in the pocket of her robe and took out another of the little devices I had seen her insert in the back of Grakker's head. "This," she said simply.

"What is it?"

She closed her eyes and swallowed hard. "It's . . . the berserk module."

"My favorite," said Grakker happily, strolling over and turning around. "Go ahead, Madame. I'm ready."

Fingers trembling, Madame Pong removed the docility module from the back of Grakker's skull. Then she inserted the berserk module. Stepping quickly away, she pointed at the side of the lunch box and cried, "Grakker! Wall bad! Kill wall!"

"Bad wall!" screamed Grakker, running forward. "Bad! Die, wall, die!"

Flexing his legs, he took a mighty leap and slammed full force into the side of the lunch box.

The entire box shook with the impact.

"Die wall!" screamed Grakker, throwing himself against the plastic once more.

When the wall didn't die, or do anything else for that matter, he snatched the Barbie head from the floor. Holding it by the hair, he swung it around his head and smashed it against the wall, screaming, "Kreegah! Kreegah, bundolo!"

Smash! Smash! Smash! Barbie was taking a beating, but the wall didn't show a single dent.

Flinging aside the head, Grakker tore off his shirt. Foaming at the mouth, he began throwing himself against the wall again. Each time he hit it and bounced away, he would run farther back, get more of a start, and try again. Soon he had a path across the center of the lunch box and was running forward, throwing himself against the side, bouncing off, running back to the far side and starting all over again, screaming all the while.

The box began to move.

Tar Gibbons and Madame Pong stood on either side of me, as if ready to protect me in case of disaster. Snout covered his eyes and turned away. Plink ran up my side; whimpering in fear, he burrowed his face into my neck.

Grakker's eyes were rolling in his head. His nostrils flared. His horns were throbbing up and down. Leaping forward, he dug his fingers into the slender crack where the top of the lunch box closed against the bottom and began to pound his head against it, screaming, "Foolish wall! Feel the wrath of the *Ferkel*'s mighty Grakker!"

"Stop him before he hurts himself!" cried Snout.

"There's no stopping him now," said Madame Pong.

Grakker let out a bloodcurdling scream. Fingers still wedged in the crack, he swung his body through his arms and began to kick the ceiling.

The box lurched forward, teetered for a moment, then fell from the table.

CHAPTER 17

Truth or Consequences

FOR A HEART-STOPPING MOMENT WE HURTLED through the air. Then we struck the floor with a crash. The box burst open, and we tumbled out.

"Run!" cried Madame Pong.

"Kreegah! Kreegah, bundolo!" bellowed Grakker, pounding his chest. "Bad wall broken! Mighty Grakker triumphs!"

Then he went racing across the room, screaming and yelling. At the same moment BKR came running into the room. As he came through the door, I realized that I was still carrying the backpack with the F/D Gizmo in it.

Where was the *Ferkel?*

I looked around frantically. There—on a table near the window. I started for it. BKR started for me. I was afraid he was going to grab me, but suddenly Grakker let out another bloodcurdling scream and used his rocket belt to launch himself into the air. Landing on BKR's head, he grabbed two of the orange spikes and began jumping up and down as hard as he could, shouting, "Booger! Booger! Booger!"

"Grakker, get off!" cried BKR, swatting at his head. Grakker only growled and sank his teeth into one of the orange spikes.

BKR screamed in rage.

I didn't stay to watch what happened next. Manipulating the controls on my rocket belt, I flew to the table where the *Ferkel* sat waiting.

Now all I had to do was figure out how to install the F/D Gizmo. I wondered if Phil's monitors could see what I was doing this close to the ship, if he would know when the F/D Gizmo was in place.

Even as I wondered this, the plant's voice came through the microphone in my pierced ear. "Rod! Climb onto the top of the *Ferkel,* and you will see a device almost identical to the one you carry. This is the F/D Gizmo for the shrinking ray. Look at it, and you should be able to figure out how the one for the enlarger should be mounted."

Behind me a ferociously angry BKR was chasing the little aliens. I started to ask Phil why I shouldn't just fly up to the top of the ship, then realized that he was afraid I would attract BKR's attention if I did.

So climb it was—not the best choice for someone averaging C minus in phys ed.

"Got you!" I heard BKR shout as I began to search for a way up the *Ferkel.* Finding a foothold, I started to scramble up the side of the ship. Behind me I heard the lunch box lid slam shut. "This time stay in there!" shouted BKR.

Who had he captured?

No time to figure that out, Rod. Keep climbing!

Reaching for another handhold, I missed, slipped down. Lying flat on my back, gasping for breath, I wished that for once in my life I didn't have to be such a clod.

Pushing myself to my feet, I started to climb again.

I fell at the same spot. I was about to use the flying belt, and take my chances on BKR spotting me, when I remembered a day long ago when my father had taken me rock climbing. Well, had *tried* to take me rock climbing. I had refused because I was afraid of hurting myself. But I had watched him very carefully from my spot on the ground. Now I remembered how he had groped for each handhold, making sure it was solid before he went farther.

I started again, working carefully.

This time I made it.

Scrambling over to the F/D Gizmo that was already in place, the one that worked with the shrinking ray, I pulled the one for the enlarger out of my backpack. I could see where it was supposed to go, and it only took a moment for me to see how I should insert it. But before I could do the job, BKR cried, "Stop right there, Rod!"

I looked up. BKR was on the other side of the room. He was holding one hand behind his back; in the other hand he held a ray gun. It was pointing straight at me. This was no tiny, ear-piercing-size ray gun. In fact, given my own current size, it was more like a ray cannon. Despite the fact that I was currently a pretty tiny target, I figured odds were fair that (a) BKR was a good shot, and/or (b) his gun had some sort of never-miss technology. Fear trickled through my veins.

"What are you up to, Rod?" asked BKR. "Trying to get back inside the ship?"

"No," I said honestly.

He narrowed his eyes. Looking straight at me, he asked suspiciously, "Rod, is there still a crew member in there?"

My mouth went dry. It was cookie-in-the-throat time.

"Well?" he coaxed. "Come on, Rod—I know you never lie. So tell me the truth. Is there someone inside the *Ferkel* who can operate it?"

I tried to swallow but couldn't. My hands trembled. I thought of Phil. I thought of Grakker and the others. I thought of my mother, weeping in the night because my father had lied to her. I thought of Little Thing One and Little Thing Two, hanging in the air above a pit filled with fire.

Looking at BKR, I said, "Of course there's no one inside."

I had done it; I had lied to him!

Unfortunately, it did me no good.

"I don't believe you!" he cried, pulling his other hand from behind his back.

He was holding Madame Pong!

"Tell me who's in the ship, Rod," he said, his voice cold.

He didn't need to tell me what he would do if I didn't tell him the truth.

"Phil the Plant," I said without hesitation.

BKR's eyes widened for a moment, and I could see he had figured out how he had been fooled.

"And what is that thing you have in your hand?" he asked.

"The device that will allow the ship to enlarge again," I said quietly.

"I think you'd better drop it, don't you?" he

asked, extending the hand that held Madame Pong and making as if to squeeze her.

"Don't, Rod!" she cried. "Put it in, put it in now!"

"Make one move and I squeeze," snarled BKR. "Hard!"

"Animal!" shrieked a tiny voice.

It was Tar Gibbons. It came racing across the floor, its four legs moving so fast they were nearly a blur. "Hee-yah! Frizzim spezzack!" cried the tiny Master of the Martial Arts as it hurled itself against BKR's ankle. It was like a hamster

attacking a Saint Bernard. Yet to my astonishment, BKR tottered and fell forward with a crash. The ray gun flew out of his hand and skittered across the floor.

I was about to slam the F/D Gizmo into place when BKR raised himself to his knees. "Rod," he cried, "stop right there! I know what happened to your father! Put that down and I'll tell you."

CHAPTER 18

Growing Pains

I FELT SOMETHING IN MY STOMACH, A SURGE OF hope and fear and anger unlike anything else I have ever experienced.

"You don't know where my father is," I said, my voice shaking.

"Oh, yes, I do," said BKR, inching forward.

I looked around for help. Tar Gibbons was lying on its side near BKR, eyes closed, legs stiff. Was it dead or merely unconscious from the force of BKR's fall?

At first I couldn't see Madame Pong at all. Finally I spotted her, sprawled on the floor about five feet from BKR. Like Tar Gibbons, she was unconscious—or worse.

Grakker and Snout were nowhere to be seen.

One, at least, was in the lunch box. The other was missing.

I was alone, face to face with the cruelest person in the galaxy.

And he was offering me my heart's desire, if I would only betray my friends.

I blinked.

Friends? When did I start thinking of them as friends? It didn't matter. I knew it was the right word.

But it didn't change what BKR was offering me.

My father . . .

"I can take you to him," whispered BKR, creeping forward. "Give me that piece, and I'll tell you all about it."

I said nothing.

"He's waiting for you, Rod," said BKR. "Waiting for you out there. I can take you to him. And I can show you things, Rod. I can show you the stars. I can take you where you belong."

It was ridiculous. BKR couldn't possibly know where my father was. It was as impossible as . . . as . . . as what? As aliens flying through my window? As me being two inches tall?

I shivered. Was *anything* really impossible?

If not, then maybe BKR really did know where my father was. I thought of all the lies Mickey had told me, and how I had believed every one of them. I was so gullible, so stupid, when it came to that.

Only now I understood more about lying. I had done it myself.

But my father . . .

A voice spoke in my ear. "Rod, ignore him. Insert the Gizmo!"

Some people have a conscience. I had a talking plant. But I wasn't sure if he was the best source of advice. After all, who knows how plants feel about their fathers?

BKR was still on his knees. He didn't look like the cruelest being in the galaxy now—just a weird guy with blue skin and a spiky head. But I remembered the words of Madame Pong: *"Millions have wept."*

"Rod!" called another voice. "Don't listen to him!"

It was Snout. He had crawled out from under a stool and was standing about two feet behind BKR.

"Why not?" I shouted. I was surprised to realize that I was crying. "Is he lying?"

"I don't know," said Snout. "I only know that he is cruel for the sake of being cruel. He must be stopped."

Cruel for the sake of being cruel.

What was the cruelest thing he could do to me?

Promise me my father.

"Rod!" cried BKR as he saw me move my hand. "Don't!"

It was too late. I placed the F/D Gizmo against the slot, and pushed down.

The next few moments were a blur. The *Ferkel* shot forward, throwing me off. I hit the table, hard.

"You fool, Allbright!" cried BKR. The *Ferkel* swooped near him. It paused, hovering, and the orange ray shot out from the bottom to suck in Madame Pong. BKR lunged for the ship, but it swung away in time. Banking to the left, it hovered over the inert form of Tar Gibbons. Again the ray shot down. But as Tar Gibbons floated into the ship, BKR threw himself at the *Ferkel*. He landed right on the ship. It sank toward the floor. Wobbling from side to side, it struggled over to Snout and pulled him in. BKR continued trying to drive it down, looking like someone trying to hold a beach ball under water. But while he couldn't get the ship all the way to the floor, neither could the *Ferkel* rise high enough to pull me in from the table.

Phil's voice sounded in my ear again. "Rod, get out of the house as fast as you can!"

"How?" I cried. Before he could reply, I figured out the answer on my own: the rocket belt.

Touching the controls, I shot into the air.

"Get back here, Pudge-Boy!" screeched BKR as I shot over his head. But he couldn't hold on to the *Ferkel* and chase me at the same time, and he wanted the *Ferkel* more. So he let me go.

My problem now was, go where? How could I get out of the house? I flew to the top of the room and looked around. The windows were all closed. I was sure that was true for every room in the house. Nor would there be any doors open.

Then I saw it: the fireplace.

I just hope the damper is open! I thought as I zoomed down over the top of the fire screen, then curved up inside the chimney. I could see blue above me. Twisting the controls, I shot straight up the chimney and into the sky.

I was barely past the bricks when I heard a rumble beneath me.

The *Ferkel* was enlarging!

I continued upward as Billy Becker's house exploded. Bricks, boards, and bits of glass went flying in all directions. I stared down in awe. Where there had been a house but moments before there was now a ship—the *Ferkel,* in its full-size glory.

CHAPTER 19

Sick Bay

AFTER A MOMENT A RAMP EXTENDED FROM THE SIDE of the *Ferkel*. Snout, now full-size, stepped out and called, "Rod! Rod, where are you?"

"Here!" I cried, flashing down to hover in front of him.

As I floated there, I had a sense that something about the alien wasn't quite as I had expected. But I couldn't figure out what it was.

"Thank goodness you're all right," he said. "Quick, fly over by that tree so Phil can enlarge you."

I shot off in the direction he pointed. Almost instantly an orange ray shot out from the top of the ship. I could see that it came from the device I had installed, which was now several times larger than me.

The world spun. For an instant I blacked out. When I opened my eyes again, I was still floating about three feet above the ground. But now I was my regular size.

I flew back to Snout. That was when I realized what had been bothering me before. He stood only a few inches higher than my belly button!

"Did the enlarger malfunction?" I asked.

He flapped his snout at me. "No, this is my—our—regular size. We don't have time to talk about that now; we have to find Grakker and BKR and get out of here. I'm bonded to Grakker, so I should be able to locate him with my mind. But if he is unconscious, or . . ." He stopped and cleared his throat. "If he is unconscious, it will be more difficult. You look for BKR."

I nodded and started to fly in a circle above the wreckage. Though I was looking for BKR, I spotted Grakker first—or at least the lunch box that I thought held him. It was nearly flat. A tiny green arm hung from one side of it.

My heart thudding with terror, I landed and gently picked up the box. I didn't dare open it.

"Snout!" I cried. "Over here! Quick!"

He rushed to my side. When he saw the crushed box, the dangling arm, his eyes went wide and he looked so sad I nearly began to cry myself. Without saying a word, he took the box tenderly from my hands. "Find BKR," he said. Then he turned and headed for the ship.

It took me another two or three minutes to locate our enemy. He was lying in a pile of rubble about fifty feet from the ship. His eyes were closed, and he looked badly battered. Remembering that the antigravity function of the belt would extend to anything I carried, I swooped down, and picked him up, and sailed into the ship.

"Good," said Phil when he saw me come through the door. "Now let's get out of here before anyone sees us!"

He pulled in the ramp, and the *Ferkel* soared into the atmosphere.

Snout appeared at my side almost instantly. "Bring the enemy this way," he said. As I followed him from the Control Room I had to duck my head to fit through the doorway. We went to an elevator, which quickly transported us to what had to be the ship's version of the nurse's office at school. "Sick Bay," was what Snout called it.

Madame Pong and Tar Gibbons were already there, each lying on a table. Above the tables hung silvery domes from which emanated a soft blue light. Like Snout, Madame Pong and Tar

Gibbons appeared to be only about three feet tall—though it was harder to judge precisely with them lying down.

Madame Pong wrinkled her nose when she saw me. "You did well, Rod," she whispered.

"Thank you," I said softly, scared by the weakness in her voice. I wanted to go to her, but I had to get rid of BKR.

"Place him here," said Snout, indicating another of the healing tables. When I laid BKR down, Snout strapped him to the table. Then he switched on the blue light.

I went to stand beside Madame Pong. "Are you all right?" I asked.

She closed her hand over mine. "I will be, before long. These healing tables are most effective."

"Our main concern now is for our fallen companion, Captain Grakker," added Tar Gibbons.

"Where is Grakker?" I asked as a lump wedged itself in my throat.

Madame Pong made a small gesture. "Over there."

I looked where she was pointing and saw Snout standing beside a fourth table. When I went to join him, he leaned his head against my elbow and sighed.

The lunch box was open now. Inside lay the

motionless form of Captain Grakker. Next to him was poor, tiny Plink, no bigger than the last joint on my pinky finger.

I reached toward them, then drew my hand back. As I watched, Grakker's eyes fluttered open. "Bad wall!" he whispered. "Bad! Kreegah!"

Then he tried to struggle to his feet.

Snout smiled and burst into tears. "He's going to be all right," he whispered.

The aliens stayed at my house that night. They shrank the ship again, which made me kind of nervous, but Phil assured us all that now that they had the missing F/D Gizmo, it would be no problem to enlarge it.

Things were pretty tense on the home front. Mom was furious with me for skipping school. I told her the truth: The bullying had gotten so bad that I just couldn't go that day.

I just didn't say whose bullying.

We were still arguing about it when the phone rang.

My mother picked it up, and by the way her face fell, I could tell it was bad news. "Yes, Mr. Markle," she said. "I'll talk to him this evening."

Hanging up, she made a face. "That was Arnie's father. He's still talking about a lawsuit. I don't know what we're going to . . ." She paused, turned away. When she turned back, her face was calm. "Don't worry about it, Rod," she said.

I appreciated the sentiment, but not worrying about it was not one of my options. Before I could think of anything to say, the phone rang again. Mom moaned and picked up the receiver.

I started to leave, but she motioned me back into the room. She listened for a minute, and if she had looked worried when Mr. Markle called, the look on her face now was of panic and disbelief. After a minute she put her hand over the receiver and whispered, "Rod, were you near the Becker house today?"

Eyes wide, I nodded.

She closed her eyes and took a deep breath. After a second she said, "The police want to talk to you."

The sergeant who came to the house was firm but kind. I could tell he didn't want to believe I had had anything to do with the explosion. I could also tell that he was afraid it would turn out that I had.

"Is it true that you skipped school today, young man?"

"Yes, sir."

"And did you go over to the Becker house when you should have been in school?"

"Yes, sir."

"Now, why would you do a thing like that?"

I can hardly remember the story I concocted—something about wanting to talk to Mrs. Becker to see if she could do anything about the way Billy was bullying me. I think it made sense, though I couldn't swear to it.

It was a good thing I had broken through my barrier about lying, because that wasn't the last whopper I had to tell before the interview was over. When the sergeant asked me if I had seen anything suspicious, I swallowed hard and lied again.

So far, I thought I was doing pretty well. But his next question really scared me.

"Is it true that you've been working on a volcano for your science project?"

No point in telling a lie on that one; everyone in my class knew what I had been making.

"Yes, sir."

"And it was really going to erupt?"

"Yes, sir."

"So you've been learning about explosives?"

"Now see here, Officer!" said my mother.

He waved his hand at her to be quiet.

"I was just going to use vinegar and baking soda," I said meekly.

"Well, that's about it for now," he said, folding

his notebook. "If you think of anything else I should know, give me a call."

It was clear that by "anything else" he meant if I wanted to confess to having blown up the Becker house.

My mother showed him to the door. When he was gone, she came back and looked at me. "Rod, do you know anything about what happened to the Becker house?"

"Yes, Mom, I do," I said.

"Something you didn't tell the officer?"

"Yes."

"What?"

I sighed. I might have been able to lie to BKR. I might have been able to lie to the police. But I still couldn't lie to her.

"Well, it blew up when a miniaturized alien spaceship that was trapped inside the house expanded to its full size."

"Rod, this is no laughing matter! What happened today is very serious. I think you'd better go to your room, young man. I'm very disappointed in you."

The taste of dry chocolate cookie heavy in my mouth, I sighed and trudged to my room.

"What's wrong, Rod?" asked Snout when he saw me come in. He was sitting on the edge of my science project. (We had figured this was a good place for the aliens to hang out. Since I hadn't finished repairing the hole, if we heard anyone coming, they could scramble through it and hide inside the volcano.)

"Everything," I said bitterly. "You guys have completed your mission, but my life is going right into the toilet. My mother is furious at me for skipping school today. And since I was out of school when it happened, our local police think *I* was the one who blew up the Becker house. Not to mention the fact that my science project still has a big hole in it!"

"I've been meaning to ask you about the project, Rod," said Phil. "How, exactly, were you planning to get it to school?"

"In my mother's car," I said, wondering what in the world he was talking about.

"And how were you going to get it in her car?"

"Well, the two of us would pick it up and . . . and . . ." I stopped as I realized what he was talking about. The volcano wasn't sturdy enough to be tipped sideways—and it was *at least a foot too wide to go through the door!*

It was a small thing, really, but it was the last straw. With a scream of despair I threw myself onto my bed and buried my head under my pillow.

I only meant to stay there for a minute, but suddenly everything—the lack of sleep, the wild adventures, the danger and drama—caught up with me. I felt myself drifting into a sleep I couldn't seem to resist. Even now, I don't know whether that sleep came from sheer exhaustion or from Snout practicing his "mental arts" on me.

Either way, it was deep and satisfying. But not nearly as satisfying as the next day, which was in a lot of ways the best day of my life—except for the part that was the worst.

CHAPTER 20

A Visit from Mr. Becker

THE FIRST THING I SAW WHEN I WOKE UP WAS MY volcano sitting next to me on my pillow. It was small enough to fit in the palm of my hand. Not only that, the hole was fixed, and the entire thing had been beautifully decorated.

"Wow!" I cried.

"What good is having a shrinking ray if you can't use it to help a friend?" burped Phil. He was on my nightstand, his pot floating a quarter of an inch or so above the surface. I could see Plink climbing around inside his branches.

"And wait till you see it erupt!" said Tar Gibbons. "We've added a few special effects!"

"This is great!" I said, hoping their "special effects" wouldn't convince the police that I was indeed the one who had blown up the Becker place.

"It is no more than you have earned," said Madame Pong.

"Directive 479.8.4.3.9 of the Galactic Code specifies that those who assist in operations of the GP should be rewarded for their efforts," said Grakker stiffly.

I was delighted to see the little guy up and around again.

I carried the volcano to the car before Mom was even awake. Phil flew the *Ferkel*—and its enlarger ray—around to meet us.

"I'd suggest we take it to about 85 percent of original size," said Snout. "That should make it easier to move around."

It fit easily into the trunk.

"This is great, guys," I said. "I don't suppose you have any advice for me on how to deal with Arnie. . . ."

Madame Pong smiled. "Just go to school and have a good day, Rod," she said.

"But . . ."

Her smile grew even broader.

"I can almost guarantee it will be a good day," she said.

And that was all I could get out of her.

* * *

Mom drove me and the volcano to school. The silence in the car was deafening. She didn't speak until we were in the school parking lot.

"Rod, about Arnie . . ." she started.

"Don't worry," I said, hoping the aliens wouldn't make a liar out of me. "I'll take care of it."

I had hoped for some reaction to the volcano when I brought it into the classroom, but people were so wound up talking about the explosion at the Becker house that they barely noticed it. About the only one who said anything was Arnie Markle. He walked over, making a point to show me the big cast on his hand, and said, "Great volcano, Allbright. I can't wait to see it go off. Where's that little guy you're supposed to give me?"

Before I could answer, the classroom door swung open. To my astonishment, Billy Becker's father—or, more precisely, the android Billy had used as his fake father—walked in.

"Good morning, Mr. Becker," said Miss Maloney nervously. "I was so sorry to hear about the terrible tragedy at your house yesterday afternoon. Is Billy all right?"

"He's fine, Miss Maloney," said Mr. Becker. "I wonder if it would be all right if I addressed the class for a moment?"

She furrowed her brow but then said, "Be my guest."

"Thank you," said the android. Then it turned to face us. "I feel I must apologize to all of you for the things you have suffered at my son's hands over the last several months. He is a very troubled boy.

"As you know, there was an accident at our home yesterday, and it was destroyed. I have heard some speculation that Rod Allbright might have been involved, both because he was out of school yesterday, and because he has been making a volcano. This is total nonsense. What happened yesterday was *entirely* Billy's fault. Let this be a lesson to the rest of you not to play with matches."

Furrowing his brow, "Mr. Becker" walked between the desks until he reached the one where Arnie Markle sat. Leaning over Arnie, he said, "I understand that you were good friends with Billy; that you almost idolized him."

Arnie nodded, uncertain of what to say.

The Mr. Becker android shook his head sadly. "You must be a very sick and troubled boy. I would suggest that you get counseling immediately. Otherwise, it is likely that you will end up in the same reform school where we have been forced to send Billy."

Arnie turned white.

"Furthermore," said the Mr. Becker android, turning back to the front of the room, "it should be clear that Wednesday's playground incident, the one in which this young man broke his hand, was entirely the fault of himself and my son, and that Rod Allbright is completely blameless in the matter. I have already spoken to Mr. Markle and made it clear that Billy has made a statement absolving Rod of all blame. This will be filed with the police." Turning back to Arnie, he added, "Your father has dropped the lawsuit. I do not think that I would want to be you this afternoon."

Arnie groaned and slid down in his seat.

Turning to me, "Mr. Becker" winked. Then he strode out of the room.

That afternoon the twins and I went out to Seldom Seen to say goodbye to the aliens. This was the bad part of the day. To my astonishment, I realized that I didn't want them to go!

They were full-size again—which is to say they stood slightly higher than my navel.

("This is fairly standard size throughout most of the galaxy," Madame Pong had told me the night before. "It is one reason that BKR disguised himself as a child on your planet. It was the only way to fit in among people who have this odd tendency toward giantism."

I had remembered the time that Snout started to say, "It could also have something to do with his stat—" and Grakker had cut him off. Now I understood that he had been about to say "stature." Grakker hadn't wanted me to know their actual size because he felt that it would make them vulnerable.)

Tar Gibbons was the first to say farewell. Stretching its neck so that it could lean its head on my shoulder, it said, "This is a sad parting for me, Young Rod Allbright. I honor the Warrior Spirit within you and wish that you could travel the stars with us."

"Thank you, Tar Gibbons," I said. "I have learned much from you already."

I didn't add that over half of it made no sense at all. The half that did make sense was terrific.

"For someone made of meat, you are a fine being," said Phil, wrapping one of his tendrils around my shoulder. "I almost feel that you could be one of the family."

"Really?" I asked in surprise.

"Mostly because you're such a nut," said Phil.

I *still* couldn't tell if he was joking or not.

"Train your mind," said Snout, reaching up with his long, spindly arms to grasp my shoulders. After he had held me for a moment, he reached into the pocket of his cloak and pulled out a book. "Here, I had the computer run off a copy in your language last night."

I took the book. It was titled *Secrets of the Mental Masters*.

"I'll read it carefully," I promised.

Madame Pong was next. "Rod, if it were in my power, I would grant you your heart's desire," she said softly.

"Do you know my heart's desire?" I asked, my voice equally soft.

She nodded. "You want your father."

My throat grew thick, but I forced out the words and asked the question I had been avoiding since yesterday. "Was BKR telling the truth? Does he know where my father is?"

"I doubt it very much," she said. "You know why he said that, don't you?"

I nodded. "To be cruel."

In that much, BKR had been successful. I knew I would always wonder if he could really have told me something about my father. Even so, I didn't doubt that I had done the right thing. I think my father would have approved.

"Please take this," said Madame Pong, slipping a ring from her pocket. "The stone is from my planet. It is of great value to my heart."

I started to protest, to try to give it back to her, but she shook her head and said, "It is the mark of a diplomat to accept a gift with grace."

Then she bowed and went into the ship.

Grakker was last. He came and stood before me, his head no higher than my armpit. He stared at me for a moment, then raised his hand and made a salute.

"Well done, Deputy Allbright. Well done indeed."

Then he boarded the ship with the others.

I took the Things by the hands, and we backed away.

With a rumble the *Ferkel* lifted from the ground. An orange ray shone through one of the F/D Gizmos, and the ship began to shrink. Soon it was the same size it had been when it landed in my papier-mâché.

Suddenly it shot straight up. In less time than it takes to tell, it disappeared into the sky.

I stared after it for a long time. Then, still holding the twins by the hands, I imitated the *Ferkel,* and headed for home.

Life would be easier without the aliens around. But if I told you I wouldn't miss them, you would know that I was lying.

About the Author and Illustrator

BRUCE COVILLE was born in Syracuse, New York. He grew up in a rural area, around the corner from his grandfather's dairy farm. Halloween was his favorite holiday, his school's official colors were orange and black, and as a teenager he made extra money by digging graves—all of which probably help explain why he writes the kind of books he does. He has published over three dozen of these weird stories, including the bestsellers *My Teacher Is an Alien* and *Goblins in the Castle*.

KATHERINE COVILLE is a self-taught artist renowned for her ability to combine finely detailed drawings with a whacked-out sense of humor. She has illustrated more than twenty books, including the recent picture book *"Take Care of Things," Edward Said*. Her collaborations with Bruce Coville include *The Monster's Ring, Sarah's Unicorn, Goblins in the Castle,* and the *Space Brat* books. Katherine likes to make toys, stuffed and otherwise, and once made a dollhouse inside an acorn.

The Covilles live in a big, old brick house, along with an assortment of children, a dog named Booger, and two cats named Spike and Thunder.